I did what I had to do. I dropped the rifle, circled to my left.

It seemed like we stood there for half a lifetime, and when he moved, I drew.

He never got his gun out of his holster. I caught him in the right hand, and he hollered and reached for his other gun, and I blasted the pearl away.

I picked up my Winchester. I put my pistol back in my holster and walked toward him. He was bent over, holding one hand with the other.

It was my first gunfight, I thought it was over.

"You should've killed me," he said . . .

The Broken Land

RICHARD PERRY

St. Martin's Paperbacks

THE BROKEN LAND

Copyright © 1997 by Richard Perry.

ISBN: 0-312-95777-7

Printed in the United States of America

St. Martin's Paperbacks edition/July 1997

St. Martin's Paperbacks are published by St. Martin's Press, 175 Fifth Avenue, New York, NY 10010.

10 9 8 7 6 5 4 3 2 1

FOR ALL THE BLACK AND MEXICAN
COWBOYS WHO HAVE BEEN
WRITTEN OUT OF HISTORY

Part
ONE

CHAPTER ONE

We rode into Laredo just before sundown on the forty-third day of our journey. Nothing above us pretended to be a cloud. The sky was flat, unblinking. The horizon wore a streak of purple, and a mean sun burned on its line.

My name's Joshua Partlow, and I was hot and tired, but I sat up in my saddle. I had a brother on each side of me, Halifax on my left, Grafton to my right. In one of my saddlebags I'd stashed five thousand dollars. I had a plan to make ten times as much before the first snowfall.

Laredo wasn't much of a town. It had one street. The highest building was three stories, and if the number of saloons told a tale, folks here were fond of drinking. There was a bank with a bright green sign, and a general store had dry goods stacked in a window. I saw two Mexicans and what I took to be three respectable women with bonnets that shaded their faces. They held to the arms of suit-wearing men whose pace said they'd no place to go.

The street was hard-packed dirt. A passel of noisy kids played a game between two flat-roofed buildings. The one on the left was a post office made of adobe and flying a limp U.S. flag. Past the last building heading west, a brand-new bridge crossed a small ravine on the way to a dozen white frame houses. In the light, the bridge was yellow.

Right now, I wanted four things from Laredo. First was proper care for my horse. Second was a bath, and third, a bed with a mattress. Finally, I wanted food from a kitchen, served on a plate that was something other than tin.

Halifax and Grafton said they'd catch up with me later. They wanted to go to the Rio Grande and look at Mexico. They were younger than me, and for days seeing another country was all they'd talked about.

I told them to go on. I'd had my fill of rivers, and I could see another country in the morning.

We'd set out from just south of Springfield, Missouri, six weeks before. We were going to Texas to hire a crew and buy a herd of cattle. We'd drive the herd north, make our fortune, and then I'd take off for Montana.

For the past fifteen days, we hadn't seen a bird smaller than a hawk, or a decent tree, or a horizon near enough to get to. We'd come across the Ozarks in the deep, wet green of spring, sneaked through a corner of Indian territory into Arkansas. We crossed the Red River outside of Durant, forded the Sabine, the Trinity, and the Brazos on ferries sailed by thick-armed men who didn't have much to say. We went through Austin across the Colorado down through San Antonio, and there, on horseback, we swam the treacherous Nueces and rode into Laredo.

That was enough rivers to last me for a spell, but my brothers, like I said, were hot to see another country, so I told them to go ahead. When they got back, they'd find me in one of the saloons, smelling of store-bought soap and having a civilized supper.

Halifax and Grafton rode off, and I looked both ways. I saw the sign a couple hundred feet up the street, just past the blacksmith. I swung out of my saddle and walked my gelding. The stable door was open, and I could see through to the back where another door let in the light. A Mexican boy was sweeping the floor. When he saw me, he put down his broom, and took the reins from me. He had strong hands and some Indian blood in him. He spoke a little English. When I asked him where was the best place for my kind to stay, the Mexican boy said Dora's.

I said thanks and slung both saddlebags over my shoulder, the one with the money on the bottom. I cradled my Winchester in the crook of my arm and took off for the U.S. flag.

The post office was full of shadows that made me think of caves. A presidential seal hung on one wall and the President's picture was on another. His face stared down at me in what I took for dislike.

The postmaster wore a white shirt with sleeves rolled to the elbows. His arms were hairy, and his visor turned his forehead green.

There wasn't any mail for me. I asked him to check again. He sighed and shook his head, but he did it. His face said he'd told me so.

I said "Thanks," and went outside. The streak of purple in the sky was wider. I could see hills in the distance and a graveyard past the houses beyond the edge of town.

I wasn't looking where I was going, and I had to jump out of the way as a hawk-faced man driving a rickety wagon nearly ran me down. His hat was jammed over jug-sized ears, and he was whipping the horse like he would a thief who'd stole something he couldn't replace.

I ducked as a man flew past my shoulder and sprawled in the dirt-packed street. He wore a rawhide vest. He was mad and scared and scrambled to his feet. He had a bruise on his forehead, and his right eye would be black in the

morning. As near as I could tell he'd come out of a board-
inghouse whose name was River End. A wooden Indian
watched me from one side of its doorway, and a man
strolled out of the dark interior. He looked both ways, like
he was expecting someone who was late. He was a head
shorter than the Indian. His arms were folded, and his legs
set wide, like he was used to having his way. Everything
he wore was brown. He had a gun belt with what looked
like a brace of pearl-handled forty-fours.

I never could understand why a man needed to wear two
guns. You could only shoot one at a time, if you wanted
to hit what you aimed at.

The man with the bruise made a move as if to dust dirt
from his clothes, but he didn't. He had a belt with a silver
buckle. When the sun hit, it was brighter than white.

"You, there," the short man called. "Move out the
way."

I obliged. The short man bounced into the street, his right
hand at his gun. The man with the silver buckle was back-
ing away, hand above his holster. His eyes were blinking
and his gun hand wouldn't be still. His body moved like it
was ready for fighting, but his heart hadn't made up its
mind.

People had come out of River End to watch. They ambled out of the general store, and the cobbler's, and the
saloons farther up the street. The men had a loose, lazy
way about them, and it had been a while since the women
at their sides had been respectable.

More people arrived to make a crowd, but were careful
not to cross the line of fire. I saw a man who looked like
a preacher. He said something to the children who'd left
their game to watch. Five or six cowboys shifted as if they
were bored. The big colored man looked like he'd never
smiled. He was standing next to a man with no gun and a

heavy beard and a few Mexicans whose clothes said they might have been farmers. They stood in the Texas sunshine and no one complained of the heat.

I began to make myself ready. I heard talking that seemed to come from a distance, and I thought somebody laughed. Then it got so quiet I looked at the purple sky. What was left of the sun was fire.

When I looked again, the man with the silver buckle had figured, What the hell. He was reaching for his gun, too much arm in the motion. The short guy was good, and quick, though not as quick as I'd seen. I heard the boom of a forty-four. I heard the "whunk" sound hot lead makes when it strikes flush at twenty paces. The red wall started to build behind my eyes. I was prepared, but still it shook me. I swallowed hard, trying not to vomit or remember. The man with the silver buckle was turning, and when he hit the ground he shuddered. I was watching the fist-sized hole in his shirt. A pool spread fast beneath him, and the sinking sun made it shine.

The short man walked over and aimed and put a bullet between a dead man's eyes. He slid his gun back in his holster. He licked his lips, then stared above our heads.

I was swallowing hard, trying to keep what was happening in my stomach from climbing to my mouth, trying to keep the red behind my eyes from blinding.

"What you looking at?" the little man said.

I kept swallowing, praying the spell would leave before he made his mind up to kill me. To buy some time, I blinked. The clear part of me watched as I smiled.

"Oh," he said, "a smiling nigger. Tell me, do you dance?"

It had been a while since someone called me that. We were twelve days out of Springfield, at the mouth of the pass that would take us through the Ozarks. After that the whites we met tipped their hats, and some mumbled "howdy," just like Caesar had said they would. In the frontier, folks didn't take much to nigger-hating, Caesar had said. Life was tough, and you never knew when the man you called "nigger" might be needed to save your skin.

It would be nice to find a place where folks didn't call me "nigger," but it wasn't like I'd never heard it. I'd been a slave as a boy in Virginia, and for years I'd thought "Nigger" was my name.

But slavery was over. My daddy fought the Civil War on the Union side to end it. Abe Lincoln had spoke, and though they'd killed him for it, the fact was I was free.

I stood, watching the short man through the red behind my eyes. My not saying a word confused him. I was bigger than him, but so were most men, and I wasn't bigger by much. I measure five-foot-eight in my stocking feet, and I'm slender. I'd been taught to avoid a fight if I could, and to face it if I couldn't. But I had this problem about killing, and seeing people die. I've called it fear, but it wasn't that exactly; it was something that went a lot deeper.

"I'm talking to you," the short man barked. "You deaf?"

I'd stood long enough for the feeling in my gut to settle and the red behind my eyes to fade. I was hearing everything, the watchers shifting, my own heartbeat, and the world was sharp and clear. The short man took a step toward me, and I dropped my saddlebags and pointed my rifle just above his belt. The crowd stiffened, swelled as if holding one breath.

I said, "I ain't looking for no trouble."

"You pointing a Winchester at me, what you looking to get?"

The fact I was talking made him feel better, I could tell that from his eyes. They were big eyes, whites stained from hard living. They said he wasn't the best judge of character, and didn't have enough sense to be scared.

"I ain't aiming to get nothing," I said. "I figure a man who wastes a bullet in a dead man just bears some watching."

"What's your beef?" he said, and smiled a mean and narrow smile. "You kin to him?"

I might have been. There weren't too many coloreds I knew who didn't have some white in their family. Or whites who didn't have colored in theirs.

But I didn't say that. I said, "Not to my knowledge. Unless you go back to Adam."

"Adam? Adam who?"

"You need to read your Bible."

"A smart nigger." He shook his head, disappointed by the notion. "Smart niggers wear me out."

I didn't answer. I just lowered the barrel of my Winchester four inches below his belt.

"Yes, sir, I got to kill you to get some rest."

"Not no time soon," I said.

"You put that rifle down, we fight like men."

I looked at him. I'd gone from being a nigger to a man. It was amazing how a Winchester could change your way of thinking.

I dropped the rifle, circled to my left, and he looked like I was trying to trick him. When the purple streak was in front of me, I stopped. It seemed like we stood half a lifetime, and when he moved, I drew.

He never got his gun out of his holster. I caught him in the right hand, and he hollered and reached for his other gun, and I blasted the pearl away. Bits of it danced in the air like pain-crazed butterflies. The crowd was making ooh and ahh sounds, and a Mexican said, "*Mi Dios.*"

I picked up my Winchester. I put my Colt back in my

holster and walked toward my foe. He was bent over like he had a bellyache, holding one hand with the other.

It was my first gunfight. I thought it was over.

"You should've killed me," he said. His eyes looked like a child's whose mama had whipped him in front of his friends. His teeth were a weird shade of yellow.

"Oh?" I said. "Why?"

" 'Cause I'm going to kill *you*."

"Is that so?"

"As God is my witness."

I'd spent six weeks in the saddle, and I was tired and a little sick to my stomach. The heat was nasty, and I hadn't gotten a letter from Amelia. I'd been nearly run over by a drunk in a wagon, and I'd watched a man die in the street. I'd had enough of this mean little stranger. The proper thing to have done was to put a bullet in his head, but it wasn't in me to do it. Still, I had to do something or people would wonder if something was wrong with my heart. I'd been told about Texas. A man thought to have no heart in the evening might be dead by morning's light.

I reached my foot out, swung it. The little man went hard to the ground, no hands to break his fall. My boot heel caught him in the nose. Blood spurted all over his shirt. He had hatred in his eyes.

"You're a dead man, nigger."

Everything I'd done to that moment was calculated to hide the thing in me I sometimes see as weakness. But now I didn't think. I stepped on his left wrist. I held my rifle, butt down, and drove it into his hand. He hollered. I stepped on his right wrist and smashed that hand. He didn't holler that time. He was out cold.

I was breathing deep and slow, keeping one eye on the crowd in case he had a partner, in case someone didn't take to me standing up for myself.

The sheriff came over, a man heavier than a lawman ought to be. He had a new sand-colored hat and a badge that could use a polish. He had eyes that said he'd waited until the fighting was done. He'd grown used to living and liked it.

"What's going on here?" he asked.

"It was a fair fight," someone called from the crowd.

The sheriff pointed to the dead man. "Who did the killing?"

"That one."

The sheriff gestured to the short man who was still out cold. "Get him out of here."

"And you," he said to me, "this is *my* town. You want to prosper in it, keep your nose clean."

I nodded and bent to pick up my saddlebags.

"Where'd you learn to shoot like that?" someone asked. Surprise was in his voice and more than a little respect.

"Caesar Littlejohn."

"Littlejohn? I heard he was dead. Said Indians got him in Wyoming."

Evening was coming on. I looked at the man who'd asked about Caesar. He was standing next to a woman in a gray dress. She was staring at me, her eyes were bright, and her tongue licked at her lips.

"They didn't," I said.

Two Mexicans and two white men bent to collect the bodies. One would wake to rue the day he'd met me; the other slept forever.

Shadows moved in from behind the buildings. It wouldn't be dark for a while, but the last of the sun was gone. All the edge left me, and I felt my tired come down. I'd figured on bad weather and rivers too swollen to cross. I'd figured on snakes and days in the saddle and cattle crazed with heat. I was ready for rustlers, and maybe an

Indian or two. But I hadn't figured on this, a part in some-body else's fight, a death I'd been good enough to dodge.

Or lucky.

I heard the buzzing. I took my first deep breath of La-redo. It was hot and smelled of blood. The flies were black and crazy with drink, and I blinked and went to Dora's.

CHAPTER TWO

Dora's was a large room with wide stairs to the second floor. The bar was set against the room's far wall. On the other walls were lanterns, and two women with painted faces moved and fired the wicks into light. One of the women laughed at something a man with a crooked grin said. He said something else, and she waved it off, but you could tell she didn't mean it.

Behind the bar was a mirror. I could see the windows at my back, the swinging doors. I could see my own self, a brown-skinned man in a dark blue shirt with a small rip in the collar, a black hat that had seen better days pulled down above my eyes.

At tables to my left, men sat playing cards or drinking. The women at their sides looked clean, dressed in blue or yellow dresses. Two were pretty and slim, not yet defeated by the life they led. Another had a yellow ribbon in her hair and couldn't have been more than twenty.

I blinked. The one with the ribbon had cheekbones from China, but her lips were fuller than mine. Her brown hair was pinned up, shining. Her skin made me think of honey left out in the rain.

I'd always wondered why mixed-blood people were so beautiful. Maybe God gave it to them as a payback for what He knew they'd go through.

Our eyes met, and she smiled, shy and fleeting, and I nodded and turned away. Something moved in me, and I was missing Amelia, and wondering why she hadn't written.

Three colored men slouched at a table. They looked like they were studying the plates they'd eaten from, wondering where the food had gone, or what kind of hungry had made them eat it. Across from them, four white cowboys played cards with the grim expressions of gamblers who'd drawn to another inside straight. Past the card players, two men sat without talking, hands around their glasses, a brown bottle like a fencepost between them.

All of them knew I was there, knew what had happened. Nobody looked at me except the lovely one who'd smiled, and a plump white whore in a calico dress who tried to pretend that she wasn't.

The only body at the bar was a colored man in a green shirt, a cowhide vest, with a back as broad as a river. His feet needed a new pair of boots, and his shoulders said to leave him alone. Something about him was familiar, but I couldn't place him.

I went to the opposite end of the bar, waved and ordered whiskey. The bartender looked like it had been a couple of years since he'd had a decent meal. He wore a purple shirt with a white bow tie. Something in his throat wouldn't stop moving. He was sweating something awful, and his eyes were as wide as the sky. I was thinking that the Christian thing to do would be to ask him if he'd make it through the night, and if there were next of kin he wanted notified, when he cleared his throat and said he'd be pleased to serve

me. *Very* pleased, but he'd have to do it from the other end
of the bar.

I couldn't tell whether he had an accent, or if fear made
his voice sound strange.

"Down there," he whispered, and pointed to the colored
man with a back like a muddy river.

Caesar hadn't told me about this. But then, of course,
Caesar had never spent time around towns of much size.
He'd been out in the Indian territory where folks weren't
civilized.

I was trying to figure out what I was feeling. I wondered
where my anger was, and why the insult felt like nothing
more than a trifling bother, like a stone in your boot and
you in a hurry to get to your true love's arms. What I
should have done was point my Winchester at his throat
and repeat my order. When I look back on it, I figure I
gave in because I'd spent forty-three days in a saddle, and
I hadn't gotten a letter from Amelia, and I'd had to think
quick on my feet so as not to kill a man. I wanted a drink,
not another fight. As long as the liquor came out of the
same bottle, and the price didn't change, I decided I had
no quarrel.

Thinking this made me feel like you did when you drank
warm water in a strong, no-pity sun. The water made your
mouth wet, but it didn't satisfy.

The colored man at the bar was still looking as if his day
had been harder than mine. His hat was tilted back, and he
was covered with dust from his head to his boot's crooked
heels. I slid in about six feet from him, and sneaked a look
at his face. He had two lines between his eyes that rode
together in a V, like they came from too much thinking.
Now I knew why he was familiar. He'd been standing outside when the fighting took place. He was the one who'd
looked like he'd never smiled.

The bartender put a bottle and a glass in front of me. He was still sweating, but now it was with relief. I poured and raised the glass, drank deep, and almost spit on the floor. Whatever poison was in that bottle was half water. I told the bartender to give me the good stuff, and that got the colored cowboy's attention. He looked at me like he wasn't used to our folks drinking good whiskey, and I thought he'd say something about it.

But what he said was, "You should have killed him."

He said it the way a man says to a stranger "Good evening," or "It looks like rain."

I slugged the whiskey back. It hit the bottom of my stomach like a fist, then spread a warmth. I could feel the tight inside me easing.

"Maybe," I said. "You know him?"

"Amos Steele. Horse thief, cattle rustler, all-purpose snake. Made his name trail-bossing for cattle drives till a couple of years ago."

"Sounds like his name wasn't such a good one," I said, and the cowboy grunted in what I took for agreement.

"When Steele first started," he said, "he negotiated like everybody else for passage through Injun land. Two years ago he figured he could pass for free if he made them scared enough. Hired a bunch of gunfighters who went and burned a village to the ground. Even killed women and children."

He poured a drink from his poor man's bottle, swallowed it and scowled. "But Injuns don't scare easy. Rumor is they got a knife with his name on it, and a place set up for his scalp. Word got to Steele, and he ain't been that way since."

"Just your average upstanding citizen," I said.

It took him some time to figure out I was joking, and then he still didn't smile. He said, "Anyways, you should've killed him. 'Cause he'll sure come back for you."

"Not with those hands."

"If he don't heal, then one of his boys'll do it for him."
He rubbed at the dust on his chin, and some fell like white
rain on the bar. "Don't know what he's doing this way.
Heard he was holed up in El Paso. Heard he'd gone to
robbing banks."

Something moved on my right, and I turned. The bartender was wiping his face with a handkerchief.

The man next to me said, "That sure was some shooting.
You really taught by Caesar Littlejohn?"

"Yup. You know him?"

"I never met him, but my pappy did. Ran into him up
in South Dakota. Said wasn't no man better with a Colt or
a rifle, black or white, and he could track just as good as
an Injun."

"I reckon that's true."

He stuck his hand out. "Bradford Chilworth," he said.
"From over Nebraska way."

"Joshua Partlow. Missouri. Outside of Springfield."

I pushed my bottle toward him. He looked at it like it
was something he shouldn't drink before he washed. He
looked like he was afraid to get used to the finer things in
life. Finally, he reached for the whiskey like he was sneak-
ing up on it, and when he poured his hand wasn't steady.
He held the glass to his lips and closed his eyes. He looked
like he'd been blessed by a God he'd just now begun to
believe in.

He asked me what brought me this way, and I told him
I was looking for cattle, that me and my brothers aimed to
buy us a herd and drive it north. After that I was heading
to Montana. My brothers hadn't made up their minds what
they'd do.

"Why Montana?"

"My daddy went and told me about it. Ever since, it's been my dream."

Bradford grunted. "You ever been on a drive?"

"No. But I can ride and shoot and rope, and so can my brothers. We aim to hire the best damn crew we can find. I'll put the word out in the morning."

"You won't find nobody better'n me," Bradford said. "Been driving cattle for seven years, back before the railroad they just put in goes all the way to Denver. Spent the winter mending fence for a rancher over near Eldorado. Just as soon as the first thaw came, I saddled up and moved on."

"You looking for work?"

"All the time."

"How do I know you're as good as you say?"

"You can ask around if you want to. I ain't in the habit of lying."

I thought about it for a second, and then I trusted my instincts. I told him if he was interested, he could be my foreman, put the crew together, buy the cattle and supplies.

He said, "My going price is one hundred fifty dollars a month."

"I'll give you one hundred twenty-five."

"One hundred forty."

"One hundred thirty."

"I'll need an advance."

"An advance?"

He nodded. I went in my saddlebag, gave him a twenty-dollar gold piece. He bit it, then shoved it into the pocket of his shirt.

"How much you paying the cowhands?"

"Thirty dollars a month."

"That's fair. The cook?"

"Seventy dollars."

He shook his head.

"How much?"

"Eighty-five."

"For a cook?"

"It's money well spent," Bradford said. "He's got a tough job. Got to feel he's paid what he's worth, or you got your hands full with problems. Cowboys get real mean if they ain't fed right. Any bonus?"

"Five dollars a man if we lose less than fifty head."

He nodded. "How many head you aiming for?"

"Fifteen hundred."

"We'll need ten men, not counting the cook. You got horses?"

I said we'd have to buy them. I knew we'd need anywhere from sixty to seventy, so the cowboys could change mounts on a regular basis. Caesar had told me that.

Bradford said he knew of a herd about ten miles outside of town on the spread of a man named Chester. Chester would have horses, too. If we couldn't get all the cattle we needed from him, we'd cross the Rio Grande. Romero was the man we'd have to see. We'd have to watch our backs with rustlers, but Romero was about as honest as they came.

"You pick your route?" Bradford asked.

"Not yet," I said. "I know to take the Chisholm."

He said he knew that trail like the back of his hand.

I asked, "What about the Indians?"

"No problem. We'll pay to go through."

"Any way to go around them?"

He shook his head. "A few years back some folks took a mind to go in through Louisiana up to Arkansas, but they ended up with range cattle trying to climb the Ozark mountains. Lost three-quarters of their herd. You aiming for Abilene or Sedalia?"

"What's your view?"

"Make it to Sedalia, you cut out half the price for ship-
ping on the railroad. 'Course, that's the hardest way. But
you make a better profit."

"Profit's what I'm interested in."

"Ain't that simple. You make a better profit if everything
turns out all right. It'll take five or six weeks longer to get
to Sedalia than to Abilene. You got the cost of your men.
You got to cross more rivers, and hope the weather holds.
You got to hope the extra miles don't eat the weight off
your cattle." He squinted at me. "You do know you sell
'em by the pound?"

If that was bait, I wasn't biting. I nodded. "What would
you do?"

"Go to Abilene. Add five hundred head, take the shorter
trip."

"Fifteen hundred head's about all I can afford."

"Buy on credit. Pay off after the drive."

"A stranger can get credit?"

"A stranger can't. But I can."

"I'll think on it," I said. But I was already thinking. I
was thinking my luck was running good to have met Bradford.

I dropped money on the bar to pay for the whiskey. The
bartender was still sweating. I took a drink, and pushed the
bottle toward my foreman.

"Much obliged," he said. He poured another drink. "So,
why didn't you kill Steele?"

I blinked. He was kind of direct. I said, "I prefer not to
kill a man unless I have to."

It wasn't the whole truth, and I thought he suspected as
much. But he let it be. Maybe he figured you didn't con-
tradict a man while you were drinking his good whiskey.
Especially when he'd just given you a job.

I arranged for a room, took my bottle upstairs, stowed

the saddlebags under the bed. I waited while a woman poured hot water in the tub. She wasn't bad looking, kind of narrow in the hips, and what looked like a razor scar beneath her left ear, but she had a pleasant face, and smooth skin the color butter gets a minute short of freezing. We looked at each other longer than we should have, and she shrugged and left the room.

The thing moving inside me was a reminder that I hadn't prayed today. Or the day before. The truth was that it had been more than a week. I told myself I'd do it later.

I kept what was moving in me quiet, took off clothes stained with this wide, wide country, and stepped into the tub. When I was used to it, I sat down, and let the water take me. Few things on God's green earth were better than a hot tub after a forty-three-day journey.

I began to think about Amelia. We were sitting on our porch at sundown, the kids put safe to bed. Our land spread away from the porch steps as far as the eye could see. The sky was as clear as a promise. In my dream I took Amelia's hand, and she looked at me, and we got up and went inside.

Amelia is my heart, my comfort. When I hold her standing up, our eyes are level. She makes me think of a willow. She's the color of a walnut. I can't describe her smell except to say it's warm and lives for a while inside me. She wears her hair pulled to a bun at the back of her neck. In my dream I reached, and the hair came down like a coal-black waterfall.

That thing moved in me again, and I told it to be quiet, and it said it might, but I'd have to stop that kind of thinking. So I thought of other things. I thought of my daddy moulding in the ground, my mama in Missouri, Caesar, who was looking after her, my brothers who ought to be back by now, and how all of us were free.

We hadn't always been. Like I said, I was born in Virginia. Before I was old enough to walk, Marse Bill Partlow, the master's son, took my daddy and some other slaves and lit out for the territory to see if it was fit for living. They'd gotten as far west as Colorado, where they came upon mountains that reached to heaven's floor. Not knowing how to get over, figuring finding a way around might take forever, they turned north, crossed Wyoming, went a hundred miles into Montana before they headed home.

The country was just too big, Marse Bill had said, too open. A man needed boundaries, horizons near enough to touch. He came back through Missouri, staked out three hundred acres of rich farmland seventy-three miles southeast of Springfield. Then he returned to Virginia to get his father's blessing, and when he had it, he headed back to Missouri. This time, my whole family went with him.

So I grew up mostly in Missouri. It was there my brothers were born. All during my growing my daddy told me stories about the territory, the herds of buffalo, the Indians, the forests with game of all variety, the rivers so thick with fish you could catch them with your hand. He said everywhere you went you came across coloreds, that many lived with Indians, had married up, and sometimes they were chiefs.

Having been a slave, it was understandable that my daddy had a different sense of boundaries than Marse Bill did. That's why he loved the little of Montana that he'd seen. Montana was all sky, my daddy said, and one day he was going back there. The land that made his master long for horizons made *his* body feel real free. My daddy had a habit of holding his arms wide when he said this, and turning in a circle.

And then the War Between the States came, and Marse Bill went off to fight and took my daddy with him. I saw my daddy one more time, a year before the war was over. He slipped into the farm under cover of darkness. He had to sneak 'cause he'd taken to fighting on the Union side. Lots of colored had, my daddy said, and everywhere the South was burning, and our folks filled the roads, sometimes with nothing more than the clothes they wore on their backs.

When my daddy left that time, I never saw him again. Don't know where he fell, or how, or where they buried him. Marse Bill didn't come back either. He took a bullet in the throat in Gettysburg, and his wife carried her children home to Virginia to be with her folks. Before she did she told us Abe Lincoln had made us free, and she left the deed to the land in our name. That deed's still between the pages of my mama's Bible, along with the birth dates and death dates of all the colored Partlows we'd ever known.

So we ended up free, and with three hundred acres of prime farmland to boot. One day me and my brothers were in St. Louis and we learned how much money there was to be made in cattle. We were grown men and looking for a way to be on our own, and Amelia had promised to marry me, and I was all the time dreaming of Montana. Money was all that was standing in the way of me making my dream come true, and Mama let me and my brothers sell off a piece of the farm to stake the drive. She wasn't too happy about it. But she respected Caesar, who'd said a man had to follow his desire or there wasn't much sense being free.

Caesar had showed up a year after the war started, wearing moccasins and a deerskin hat, and a limp from an Apache arrow that had gone clear through his knee. He told stories richer than my father's about a wilderness so unspoiled just to look would take your breath. . . .

Someone was knocking. I reached for my gun, and the

door was coming open. I aimed about four feet off the floor and waited. The lovely girl stepped inside. The room grew small, and I thought what a miracle that a neck so delicate managed to hold up her head.

She looked at the gun. If she was worried, she didn't show it.

"Your brother sent me," she said.

I stared at her. I wanted to ask where'd she come from, how she got to be so lovely.

"No, thanks," I said.

I heard a commotion behind her, and the door swung wide, and there was Halifax, all six foot one, two hundred pounds of him. He had a whiskey bottle in one hand, and a wild-looking gal riding his back.

Grafton was behind him, laughing. He was an inch shorter than Halifax, but ten pounds heavier. Whatever size I hadn't got, they had.

"Hey, big brother," Halifax said. "We's done seen another country."

"It looks just like Texas," Grafton said.

I looked at them. They both were drunk.

I said, "You take care of your horses? We're riding in the morning."

"We riding tonight," Halifax said, and the woman on his back said "Giddy-up."

"You're gonna need your wits about you," I said.

Grafton grinned. When he did he looked younger than he was.

He said, "Man don't live by work alone, big brother. The horses is tended to. And morning's yet to come." He winked. "I'll be next door. Halifax's down the hall. You taking this one?"

I looked at the lovely girl. I shook my head.

"Then come with me," he said, and grabbed her by the hand.

Halifax was staring at the girl. The whore on his back put both hands over his eyes.

Grafton said, "Say hello to Amelia for me," and laughed. He had the decency to shut the door behind him.

I got out of the tub, put on fresh clothes I'd carried from Missouri. I emptied and cleaned my pistol, reloaded it. I wiped my Winchester down, then slung the saddlebag with the money over my shoulder, and went to get some supper. I ate stew beef and drank good whiskey until the room began to turn. I met Dora, a tall white woman in a wine-colored dress that went from her chin to her ankles. She had light brown hair, a funny smile, and she shook hands like a man.

I went upstairs, got into bed. I could hear Grafton and the women in the room beside me, the older one who had some Indian in her, the young one with skin like honey. How'd she get to be so lovely, and what was it like to be with her?

It felt strange to think of my brother with a woman. But Grafton was a man, only a year younger than me, and three years older than Halifax, although I thought of them as much younger.

I pulled the covers over my head and hummed to shut the noise out. I tried to rest on my stomach, but I had to turn on my side. I thought of cold winds whistling across a midnight landscape, lakes wearing ice, snowfalls, the deliverance in prayer. I didn't want to pray. I didn't know why I didn't.

I tossed and turned some more. Finally I slept till morning's early light.

CHAPTER THREE

In the morning I told my brothers what Bradford had said, that we had a better chance at increased profits by taking the shorter drive to Abilene and buying another five hundred head on credit.

Halifax said, "How we get what we owe back to Texas?"

I said I'd have to ask.

When Bradford came down to breakfast, I introduced my brothers to him. He'd shaved and beat some of the dust from his clothes. The lines between his eyes still moved toward one another, but they didn't meet. Maybe the lines didn't touch when he'd gotten a good night's sleep. Or maybe he'd used some of his advance to sample one of the whores.

When I asked him how we paid back the credit, he said the man we owed would send a cowhand with us. When the drive was over, we'd send the money back by him.

"Let's head out," Bradford said. "We got to buy some cattle."

He stood up, took a step, and stumbled. I looked at his feet.

"New boots," I said.

They were deep brown with stitching like an arrow on the toe. The way he was standing made me wonder if they were too small.

Grafton said, "They're pretty enough to sleep with."

"I ain't slept with no boots." Bradford scowled. "I bought these here this morning."

Grafton said, "You got boots this time of morning?"

Bradford nodded. "I woke the cobbler up."

Grafton and Halifax and me were grinning.

"I don't see nothing funny," Bradford said.

We saddled up and headed west out of Laredo, across the brand-new bridge over the dry, cracked bed of what once had been a stream. The clapboard houses had gray smoke rising from their chimneys. Past the houses the graveyard was staked with crosses, and at our back the morning sun.

We rode across land that was tan and marked by cactus stiff as soldiers at attention. In the distance a gathering of mesas wore tops that were stained deep red. There were cattle skulls bleached and empty, and to the north, a butte soared like a totem to an unknown Texas god.

We rode, and the land climbed into hills, on the other sides of which were hollows that had once been grazing holes. Bradford said that cattle once had roamed wild here, that they'd grown to be so many they'd exhausted food and water. But a few of these grazing spots were still around, and it was toward one we were headed.

We moved toward mesas that kept their distance like bashful strangers. We came to the top of another hill, and all of us rode carefully. The hill's bottom was at a drop of maybe fifty feet. Two cabins sat off to one side. Across from the cabins slumped three lean-tos, and a corral with thirteen horses. Beyond that, watched by men who looked asleep on horseback, was a middling herd of longhorns. Some were grazing, and some were folded on the ground.

I guessed there were about five hundred head, and maybe not that many. If we could buy these at a reasonable price, we'd have to find a place to hold them until we found fifteen hundred more.

It wasn't convenient, but it would be a start.

We found the trail that snaked down the sandy hillside. We rode into the camp, and out of the cabin came a man squinting at the morning. He hadn't finished putting on his clothes. His suspenders hung in loops and his once-white shirt was open. Instead of boots, he wore rawhide sandals. He had toenails like a rooster's, and his belly was still looking for a meal it didn't like.

"This here's Chester," Bradford said.

We said our "howdies," and Chester yawned, and we got down off our horses.

"We looking to buy some cattle," Bradford said. "Two thousand head."

"You late," Chester said, and spit tobacco juice six inches from my boots. "Just drove close to eighteen hundred up to Crystal City. Couple of fellas from Kansas bought 'em all."

I said, "What do you want for what's left?"

A yellow dog pranced over, shaking and begging for love. Chester kicked at him, and he scurried away and wagged his tail like a sad woman waved good-bye.

I didn't hold with mistreating animals. Maybe it was in my face what I was feeling, 'cause Chester's eyebrows rose as sharp as his deadly toenails. I hoped he didn't take a mind to bushwhack me with his feet.

"Why don't you come inside?" he said, and yawned. "Never did like to do business in the heat."

I sent Halifax to count the head and check to make sure they were healthy. I told Grafton to watch the horses. I went inside with Bradford and the man with the dangerous feet.

The cabin had a table and three sawed-off logs for chairs. In one corner was a bed with the covers all rumpled, as if Chester had wrestled bad dreams. A potbellied cast-iron stove took up another corner. In summer it would make the place too hot to breathe in, and in winter keep you turning if you wanted both sides warm.

A coffeepot sat on the stove. On the floor a tub shone like new money, filled with pots and pans that would take a week to wash. I spent a couple of minutes trying to figure out the smell. All I could tell was it was something two days dead.

"Whiskey?" Chester said.

It couldn't have been eight in the morning. Bradford shook his head. I said, "No, thanks," and took off my hat. It was something my mama had taught me. No matter whose house you go in, always take off your hat.

We sat on the logs. Mine had a ridge in the middle about the thickness of a finger. I wanted to get this over with, get back on a saddle where my butt fit proper and I could breathe without smelling whatever it was that was dead.

"What's your price?" I asked.

Chester frowned, as if to say a man who sat down to business could be excused for not taking a drink, but hurrying the deal was bad manners. He slurped from the bottle, wiped his mouth with a hand.

"These head caused me a heap of trouble," he said, and I knew he was fixing to lie.

"If you ride about four days west, then two days north, you'll come to the spot where we found them. Little valley with the sweetest stream, and grass enough to graze a herd three times the size."

His voice got deeper, like a good preacher when he's moved himself with nothing but his words.

"These here was particular wild, maybe 'cause, as near as I could tell, they'd never seen a white man. Or maybe they just plumb didn't take to being moved out of such a pretty place. What I do know is it took eight men a day and a half to round 'em up. Then, on our way back, rustlers come down upon us. I lost a man in the fighting, and the cattle scattered, and it took a day to bring 'em together again. The third day it rained, and two days after that a dust storm tried to blow us back to Kingdom come."

He reached for the bottle, swallowed long. "Cattle give you that much trouble," he said, "you right pleased to sell them to the first man comes along. All you mean to do is get a fair price for your bother."

It was a hell of a winding road to what even a steer would have known was coming.

Bradford was leaning over, doing something beneath the table. I couldn't figure what till I saw his hand. He was wiping the dust from his boots.

I said, "What's your fair price?"

"Same as I sold the others to the fellows from Nebraska. Five dollars a head."

I could hear flies buzzing at the tub, and when I looked the dog was curled up in the doorway.

"Kansas," I said.

Chester looked at me like to say it was his stock and his story, and he could have buyers from New York if he wanted.

"What you think, Bradford?" I said.

Bradford grunted.

The going price for longhorns was four dollars a head. And that was top dollar if you bought from one of the ranches. Chester rounded up mavericks, cows that lived on the range and belonged to the first man who claimed them. He didn't have the cost of branding, or feeding them over the winter. "I'll give you three," I said.

He looked as if I'd said something awful about his people, and we spent fifteen minutes dickering. We settled on three dollars and twenty-five cents a head, when he threw in grazing rights for four days, and said we could sleep in a lean-to.

I went outside and got the saddlebag with the money. Grafton was on his haunches scratching the yellow dog's ears. Halifax came back from the cattle. He'd counted five hundred fourteen head, and no signs of diseases. I took the bag inside, and when Chester saw cash, he felt better and buttoned his shirt. He shoved the money into his pockets, and all of us went outside.

Bradford said, "We need a crew. Any hands to spare?"

"A couple. You'll have to wake 'em up. They tried to suck all the whiskey in Laredo the last few nights."

Bradford went into the lean-tos. He came out with three men rubbing sleep from their eyes. Five or six others hadn't come back from town.

I looked at the tall cowboy, the skinny one with the wiry frame. He said his name was Ebeneezer, but people called him Slim. He'd been standing in the crowd when I'd had it out with Steele. And I'd seen him last night at Dora's with a fat whore on his lap. Now he looked like he and the whore had been fighting, and she'd come out on top. He nodded at Bradford's feet. "Nice boots," he said, and Bradford stared at him till Slim, puzzled, dropped his eyes.

The other two guys were Burt, a white man with a strawberry-colored birthmark on his cheek, and Singer, a pudgy Negro boy of about eighteen who had a banjo strapped to his back.

Bradford told them the salary and the bonus. We shook

hands all around and got on our horses. We'd leave Burt and Singer with the cattle, take Slim into Mexico.

I was feeling good.

"Okay, boys," I said. "Five hundred down, fifteen hundred to go."

We spurred those horses and shouted loud enough to make the dog bark and some cattle raise their heads.

We rode, spread out in a single line abreast of one another. There were five of us going in a gallop, and we left clouds of dust behind.

An hour later, we crossed the Rio Grande at a spot where the river was shallow and wound with no resistance past brush and moss-draped trees. On the other side, the bank was thick with green misshapen things that rose like a wall before us. Beneath the river's mud-brown surface, the sun was muted gold. Here and there a dead limb floated, or a tangle of brush made its lazy way downstream.

"Watch out for snakes," Bradford said, and we entered the water. It came up to my horse's belly. I reached in a hand and the water was warm. I rubbed the wet hand over my face, and rode to the other side, scrambled up the bank, and we were in Mexico.

Grafton was right. It looked like Texas: land reaching out in all directions, the sameness broken by patches of wiry grass. As we rode we kept coming upon what in these parts passed for trees. They made me think of crippled black men with crutches stuck in the ground.

The land flowed back beneath the feet of our horses. Once Halifax and Grafton were on both sides of me, and I grinned at them. It felt good to be young and have a plan and be headed toward a future. It felt good to think that though I headed south, I was on my way to Montana.

We came to sagebrush high as my horse's fetlocks, and

we slowed to go around it. We came to a dirt road that just appeared in the earth and started for no reason. We rode until we saw buildings shimmering up ahead.

Bradford said it was a town called Nuevo Laredo, about an hour's ride away. We stopped and opened our canteens and washed away the dry.

When we rode again, I thought about how the beautiful girl had made me feel, how I'd turned away from my wanting and stayed true to Amelia. It made me feel strong and worthy, and I tried to whistle, but the wind in my face wouldn't let me. So I hummed a little to celebrate, and we came to Nuevo Laredo.

The town had a street of adobe buildings that looked flattened by the sky. Three broken wagons claimed the space where the street opened into a circle. Pigs and goats and chickens owned the rest. The animals were fat and healthy. From beneath sombreros, brown-eyed Mexicans looked at us. I saw two women with hair to their waists and shoulders bare in the sunlight. A priest in black walked close to the buildings, and the church had a cross on its top.

I remembered the promise I'd made to Amelia. I'd said I'd say a prayer every day, and for a while I hadn't done it. I glanced at the sky and thought of making up a prayer. I could thank the Father for my health and strength. I could thank Him for the health and strength of my brothers. I could ask Him to watch over us and bless us, and to help make our dreams come true.

It didn't have the kind of ring I thought a prayer should have. I was about to say it anyway, when a boy with no shirt and cut-off pants threw a rock at us, then hightailed it around a building. If I'd had the time, I'd have stopped and put him across my knee.

Five miles later the road split, and Bradford led us on

the fork that branched to our left. We rode another hour, stopped to rest at an abandoned homestead. I drank from a well with water so cold it made my front teeth ache. I looked at the house caved in to its flooring. I wondered who'd lived here, where they'd gone, and why.

We watered the horses and Bradford smoked a pipe. When he'd finished, he said to wait for him, and he rode back the way we'd come.

Me and my brothers sat on the porch step. Grafton was dozing. Halifax was drawing on the ground with a stick. He kept rubbing out the top part of the drawing.

I watched the light hug the far horizon. I was thinking how different my brothers were. Halifax had that serious way about him, a deep-seated need for privacy and a stubbornness that sometimes made him fly off the handle. Grafton loved to laugh, and moved through life as if he had a scale inside him that was perfectly balanced. Mama said they'd been born the way they were. Halifax was a colicky baby who cried at the drop of a hat. Grafton hardly cried at all.

Halifax looked up from his drawing. "Grafton," he said. "What was she like?"

Grafton opened his eyes. "What was *who* like?"

"The pretty one."

"Oh, her." He seemed to think about it. "Best I ever had."

Halifax nodded. He didn't look happy.

Grafton let him suffer for a while. Then he said, "Truth is, I didn't get it. First one wore me out, and when I woke up, both were gone. But that's okay. Means I get a free one the next time I'm in Laredo."

"I see," Halifax said. He looked like he felt better.

"Why you so interested?"

"I ain't interested," Halifax said. "I'm just passing time

with conversation. Something the matter with that?''

Grafton looked at me, and I winked.

''Want me to sell you what I got coming?'' Grafton asked. ''Give you a discount.''

''No, thanks,'' Halifax said. Then he bent and resumed work on his drawing. It looked like a bird. The wings were spread like open arms, but he couldn't get the top of the head right.

Bradford returned in half an hour. He didn't say where he'd gone, and nobody asked him. He got off his horse and hopped on one foot. He reached in his saddlebags and sat down on the ground. Then he took off his new boots, and pulled his old ones on.

We all were grinning. Those new boots had put a hurting on his feet.

Slim laughed out loud, but I bit my laughing off. Bradford had a storm growing in his face, and the V was back to touching in the space between his eyes.

''What you laughing at?'' he said. His voice was high, and veins popped in his neck. He was talking to Slim, who was bent over double, trying to catch his breath. Bradford took his gun out.

''You still think it's funny?''

''Hey,'' Slim said, and he wasn't laughing.

''Bradford,'' I said. ''Ain't no cause for shootin'.''

He acted like he didn't hear me, didn't even look my way.

''Don't laugh at me,'' he said. ''Don't *never* laugh at me.''

''Okay,'' Slim said.

Bradford said, ''Mount up. It's time to ride.''

We got on our horses. Grafton was shaking his head, and Halifax was frowning. I was remembering this morning when Grafton had teased Bradford about sleeping with his

boots, and Bradford had gotten so hot. I'd thought my foreman was just one of those men who didn't have a sense of
humor. But it was more than that, and I'd have to keep an
eye out. It was one thing not to laugh at others. It was
another not to laugh at yourself.

We rode until we came to a gully that wouldn't let us cross
for half a mile. Then we went up over a hill and Romero's
camp sprawled below us.

I'd never seen anything like it. The camp was a well-
protected hiding place hollowed out by nature. In the middle was a great house, part adobe, part wood. Shacks
burned deep brown from the sun spread in half circles
around it. The back of the house was up against the side
of a ridge. On top, a lookout framed by the sky stared down
and shifted his rifle.

We came down the hill. Children scurried into doorways,
women hid their faces. Men with drawn guns took up positions behind wagons, behind three corrals that held close
to two hundred horses.

We came in slow with our heads up and our hands out
in the open. Nobody said a word. We rode up to the front
of that house, and I made to get down from my horse, when
Bradford said to stay put. A horse snorted in the corral to
my left, and another reared and neighed. We sat, not talking, and I could feel the eyes at my back. A man came out
of the house and walked toward us. He wore his gun belt
in the way of Mexicans, like a sash across his chest.

"Romero," Bradford said.

Romero was about my height. He had on a leather som-
brero, a blue shirt and pants with what looked like silver
pieces stitched into their sides. His black boots would have
cost most cowboys a year's pay. They looked soft enough
to wash your face with, and Bradford's eyes were jealous.

Romero said "Good afternoon" in Spanish. Bradford said the same thing, and then we all were quiet. Romero spoke something else that sounded like the beginning of a song. I was thinking we were going to have a problem, since most of the Spanish I knew had already been spoken, and I knew more than my brothers. Maybe Slim could speak it. When I looked at Slim, I gave up that hope. He wore the expression of a cow who'd just been ordered to dance. But I'll be doggoned if Bradford didn't start jabbering away, like he'd talked Mexican from birth.

Following Bradford's lead, we all dismounted. We stood with our hands in clear view, one holding the horse's reins, the other at our side. Romero and Bradford were talking up a blue streak. When they both got quiet for a minute, I asked Bradford what was going on.

"Everything's fine. He's got a herd about six miles from here. We can cut out fifteen hundred."

"How much?" I said.

"Three dollars a head."

"That's fair. And horses?"

"I told him we need seventy-five. He'll give us the lot for two hundred fifty dollars."

"What about credit?"

Bradford nodded, and Romero spoke again.

Bradford turned to me. "He says we are welcome into his house. He'd be pleased to eat with us."

"That's right nice of him," I said.

We took the horses over to the wagons, tied them. I slung the saddlebag over my shoulder, and we stopped at the well to wash.

Inside, the house was cool and spacious. I wondered where Romero had gotten all the flowers. The heads were the size of oranges and were blue and yellow and red.

The next room had paintings on the wall. They were all

stern-faced Mexican men who wore store-bought suits and watched us with iron eyes.

Romero called out and a Mexican woman appeared and led us to another room. This one had wide windows for three walls and a long wooden table in the middle. A dozen large men could have eaten here and had elbow room to spare.

Three children came in, dressed in white, one a boy of about twelve, two pretty girls around five and seven. These were his children.

Romero spoke again to Bradford from where he sat at the head of the table, and Bradford translated. We would forgive the absence of his wife. She was "*embarazada*," pregnant with their fourth child.

We said congratulations.

The woman brought food to the table. Huge mounds of rice and beans. A meat that tasted like pork. A roast chicken, and ears of corn. We ate mostly in silence. Then my brothers and Slim went to fetch the horses, and me and Bradford and Romero prepared to take care of business.

I said to Bradford, "Tell him I appreciate the credit."

Romero said, "You are most welcome."

My mouth dropped open. "You speak English," I said, and when I did, I felt stupid.

Romero smiled. "I'll send two of my men with you. If anything happens to them, you, señor, will return my money. If you don't, I'll hunt you down."

I swallowed. He was still smiling. He'd said it so friendly-like.

"I'm an honest man," I said.

"I believe that."

We began to do business. When we finished, my saddle-bag was light.

We went outside. Romero pointed out the two men who

would ride with us. The skinny one was named Pedro, but everyone called him Petey. The short one was named Esteban.

Bradford spoke to each of them, and when he'd finished, I asked him where he'd learned to speak Spanish.

"My mama," he said.

I was surprised, and I'd have asked more about it, but the tone of his voice said I shouldn't.

CHAPTER FOUR

We rode east out of Romero's camp, driving the horses we'd bought. A wind sprung up, not hard, but hot, and it brought tears to my eyes. I pulled my hat low. We rode to the top of a hill, and the herd was at the bottom. It spread toward the horizon as far as I could see.

Grafton whistled. "That sure is a lot of cows," he said, and I grunted and said it sure was.

I figured about ten thousand head, a dark brown lake of longhorns. I could smell them, a kind of sour mixed with dung. The men on horseback watching the herd had turned their backs to the wind.

Romero's men led us down the hill, and told the cowhands that we'd bought fifteen hundred head. By the time we'd cut out ours, the day had an hour of light left. I thought we'd make camp back on the other side of the hill where we'd be protected from the wind, and then we'd move out in the morning. But Bradford said we'd be better off driving the herd now. We were shorthanded, and the longer we were out here, the more chance of meeting bad luck. He wanted to get back to the river tonight.

So we started to move those animals back toward the

Rio Grande. In the morning, we'd hook up with Burt and Singer at Chester's. We'd buy two wagons, stock supplies, find a cook who took pride in his trade. We'd hire the cowhand we needed. Right now we had Bradford, me and my brothers. Slim and Burt and Singer brought us up to seven, and Romero's two men made nine. Bradford said ten hands would do the job right nicely. We'd spend a couple of days branding, and then we'd be on our way.

I'd already figured out the brand, 3P, for the three Partlow brothers. I had it in my saddlebag.

Moving the herd wasn't easy. The longhorns were stubborn, and not given to moving so late in the day. They wouldn't stay together. We tried three or four steers as leads for the pack, and then we found one with some getup-and-go in him. Still we had to keep stopping to pull back the few that kept wandering off. Finally we got them going, just before dark fell.

I felt better now. The land made a deep blue line at each horizon. The sun had set and left a blood-red glow that was fading as I watched. A full moon set up house in the eastern sky, and stars were bright stones slung in the dark.

Then the wind changed, came whistling from the south. Clouds filled the sky as if the good Lord had closed a window. The longhorns were restless, swinging their heads, and their horns made clicks when they struck each other. I asked Bradford if we ought not stop, but he said if we kept going we'd make it.

I was thinking about how I had no choice but to trust the judgment of a man I hardly knew, a man with no sense of humor and a past he didn't want to talk about, when the men came out of the dark, maybe ten or so, and they took us by surprise. Later Bradford said they must have been low on the backs of their horses until they were right up on us. Then they bore down out of the night, guns blazing, hollering like something risen from the dead.

We fired back, trying to see in the dark to figure which men were ours, and we came together, and then spread out, riding the flanks of the herd. I could smell gunpowder, and the cattle were lowing, and on the rise above a cry rang out and I couldn't say it was human.

I kept firing steady at nothing I could see, emptying my Colt, reloading and firing again, trying not to think about killing someone, telling myself I had to protect myself and what I'd come to own.

I felt like I was in the middle of a bull's-eye. A bullet went by with a buzz that nearly stopped my heart. I put my head to my gelding's neck and kept shooting into the dark. I was hoping whatever I hit would have the good grace just to be wounded, but I was too scared to hope it hard.

I don't know what would have happened if the wind hadn't changed again. But it did, and the clouds began to blow away, and light from a piece of that moon lit the night, and I could see again.

And then the clouds moved all the way from the moon's big eye, and it was as bright as day, and no sound but the lowing cattle. My heart beat so fast I put a hand on my chest to slow it. I was sweating so hard I could smell myself.

I reloaded, and looked over my shoulder. The cows' big eyes were shining. I could see their noses flaring, and they were moving as if blind. All I could think was, *Please, God, don't let 'em stampede*. I knew what to do when a stampede happened, Caesar had told me. But I'd never been in a stampede, and I'd never thought about one happening at night.

The wind still blew, but not as hard. I sat on my horse, turning in a circle. The cows had started to settle. A rider came up on my left. I raised my gun, but it was Bradford.

"I think we run 'em off," he said. "You all right?"

"Yeah. You see the others?"

"Not yet," he said, and called out.

A voice answered from the other side of the herd. I heard horses running, and then my brothers came up, Halifax with his gun drawn. Grafton's hat had slid down his back, held by a tie at his neck. A moment later, Romero's men arrived.

"Everybody all right?" Bradford asked. "Where's Slim?"

"Over here," Slim said, and rode toward us.

"I think I got one of 'em," Bradford said.

"Me, too," Slim said.

Bradford said, "Slim, you come with me. See what's out there. The rest of you keep these cattle calm. Can any of you sing?"

"Like a nightingale," Grafton said.

Me and Halifax laughed. Grafton had a voice like a bull-frog.

"He'd just better hum," I said.

Bradford and Slim rode off toward the rise. Romero's men, me, and my brothers split and circled the herd. I thought about a song to sing. None that Caesar had taught me would come to mind. I'd learned songs about little doggies and the Chisholm Trail, but I couldn't remember a word. So I sang "The Battle Hymn of the Republic" and the cattle liked it fine.

While I sang the wind blew soft and the cows were quiet. The full moon lit up the world, and the man in its face was smiling.

Bradford and Slim came back with two of the crooks who'd bushwhacked us. One was walking, hands tied together. The other was slung across his horse's back. I heard him moan.

"Got two of 'em," Bradford said. "The others run off like the thieving skunks they is."

I said, "Any idea who they are?"

He shook his head.

"I figured they was riding with Steele."

Bradford said, "They'd have to have trailed us out here, and nobody did. I doubled back when we stopped before, on our way out to Romero's. Besides, Steele wouldn't ride with but a few men. When he comes he'll bring an army."

"Where you think these come from?"

"They won't say. My guess is they was planning to hit Romero's men at nightfall. Then we came along and they figured we was easy pickings."

Halifax said, "What'll we do with them?"

"Hang 'em."

I said, "Hang 'em?"

"Yup."

Grafton said, "We're going to hang two *white* men?"

Bradford glared at him. "They got a neck, don't they?"

I said, "Why don't we turn 'em over to the sheriff in Laredo?"

"'Cause that's Texas," Bradford said. "This here's Mexico, and Laredo sheriff got no . . . *whatyoumacallit* here."

"Jurisdiction," I said.

Bradford looked at me. "Even if he did, it's range law. Rustlers hang. You don't, they encouraged all the more."

"I don't like it," I said, and he turned away, like I wasn't there, or he hadn't heard what I'd said.

I didn't want to buck the law of the land, but I wanted no part of a hanging. For me, it didn't have anything to do with the rustlers being white. I'd seen a man hanged, a long time ago, when I was a boy in Virginia. The man was colored, and they said he'd sassed a white gal. The master made us watch. I was on my daddy's shoulders, high above the crowd, feeling like a giant. Just before they set the man on fire, my daddy hid my eyes.

I looked around, over the backs of the cattle. The land stretched featureless in all directions except for the hump-backed hills and those trees that clawed like the hands of black men trapped in shallow graves.

I said, "Where we gonna find a tree suitable for hanging?"

Bradford said, "We'll find one before we get to Texas. Now let's move out."

We rode for a couple of hours, and we came to a grove plopped like a pond in a desert, though the trees, while bigger than we'd seen, still weren't much for size. They sure weren't nothing like the ones back home, and I wondered if they'd hold a grown man's weight.

I tried not to think about having to hang a man, in this case two men. I hadn't really looked at them until now. The one who'd walked back into camp was short and skinny, with a scar above his right eye. He hadn't shaved in a couple of days. The other, the one who'd been grazed across the forehead, was older, a lot of muscle in his shoulders.

"Joshua," Bradford said to me. "We need your horse."

"My horse? For what?"

"We got two men to hang. And one horse."

I started to tell him to use somebody else's, but I swallowed and swung to the ground. My legs felt funny.

Bradford put the rope around the short rustler's neck. Slim and Grafton got him on my horse with his hands tied behind him. They did the same to the man with the muscle in his shoulders. Then they led them under a tree, looped the ropes twice over the tree branch, and stepped behind the horses. Grafton gave his end of the rope to Bradford, and Bradford and Slim held the ropes in their hands.

"Joshua," Bradford said. "Halifax. Stand over here."

Me and Halifax moved to where he pointed.

"When I give the word," Bradford said, "you send them horses forward."

I stood, thinking I'd never been near a horse that smelled so bad. Then I realized it wasn't the horse. It was the man with the scar above his eye. He'd messed himself. He was crying. Not a hard cry. A steady one. I looked away.

"Now," Bradford said.

Halifax slapped the horse. It jumped forward and stopped. The man with the muscle was swinging, making choking sounds.

I didn't move.

"Do it," Bradford barked, and I hit the horse with my fist on his rump, harder than I had to. The horse kind of went three ways, and then it went forward, and the man who'd messed himself screamed. It sounded like "Jesus, Mama," and then it stopped. Veins were popping in his face, and his eyes looked like a frog's.

I turned my head. Grafton was looking at the ground. Halifax was staring in the direction of the cattle. I'd planned to just keep turned until it was over, but the tree limb snapped, and both bodies fell, and the rustlers sprawled on the ground.

"God dang it," Bradford said.

He and Slim still held the rope in their hands, and Slim was laughing.

"We got to find another tree," Slim said, still laughing.

"The hell we will," Bradford said. "We shoot 'em."

Bradford scowled at Slim. "You'd laugh at anything," he said. "You'd laugh at . . ." He couldn't find the word for it.

"Help me get 'em up," he said.

Bradford and Slim pulled the men to their feet. The muscled man had fury in his eyes. The short man was steady crying.

"All of you," Bradford barked, "stand over here."

Me and Slim and Halifax stood next to him. Grafton was on my other side. Bradford took out his gun. "On three," he said, "we shoot 'em."

In the middle of trees, in a moonlit Mexico, we took out our guns. Mine was still warm. Bradford ripped the shirts off the rustlers' bodies. He tore a piece for each of us. We wrapped our guns so the shots would be muffled and wouldn't spook the herd.

I could feel the sickness in my stomach. I could see the red wall build behind my eyes.

Grafton said, "Ain't we supposed to ask them if they got anything to say?"

"Hell, no," Bradford said. "Get ready. We fire on three. One . . . two. . . ."

I wasn't shooting nobody. I aimed above the doomed men's heads and fired into the night. I heard the bullets strike the rustlers. Then it was quiet.

"Okay," Bradford said. "Bury 'em."

I was sick to my stomach and nobody had a shovel. We had to use our hands and rocks and sticks. We dug graves beneath the tree whose limb had broken. The only thought I let myself have was that justice was hard work.

When the graves were dug we put the dead men in them. We covered them up and stacked rocks to keep the animals away.

Bradford said we had to leave a sign saying what we'd done and why.

He asked, "Can anybody write?"

"I can," I said.

Bradford got a Bowie knife from his saddlebag. It was

big and smelled of something oily. It was razor sharp and in the moonlight it shone like a broken promise.

"What should I say?"

"Just tell what happened."

I thought about it for a moment. I'd been in these parts for little more than a day, and three men had died in my presence. At this rate half of Texas would be buried before I got back to Missouri.

I went to work. The tree was dry and soft and the knife was sharp and the writing easy. I carved: RUSTLERS. THE TREE BROKE, SO WE SHOT 'EM.

I asked, "Do we say who we are?"

Bradford said we didn't.

It was just as well. It would be my luck that someone would come along who'd recognize my name, and word would find its way to Amelia about what I'd played a part in. And that would be the end of everything I dreamed of, for I knew what would happen if Amelia found out.

I pushed aside those thoughts, mounted my horse, and we moved those cows and seventy-five horses. We came to the Rio Grande, and Bradford held his hand up.

"What's the problem?" I asked. "Why are we stopping?"

"Got to wait here till sunup," Bradford answered. "Cattle won't cross a river 'less they can see the other side."

I shook my head. There was so much I didn't know.

We stayed there for what was left of the night. Every time I closed my eyes, I saw the faces of dead men. Finally, I gave up trying to sleep and stared into the dark. I watched as the sky grew light, a glow with the softness of whispers. When the sun came up we found a place where the water was shallow, and we crossed the river to Texas.

CHAPTER FIVE

When we got back to Chester's, we corralled the horses. We put the herd out to pasture with the five hundred we'd bought less than twenty-four hours before. My body was tired and my spirit troubled, but when I looked at the longhorns in the sunlight, I felt a little better.

Halifax and Grafton volunteered to watch the herd while Bradford and I got some shut-eye. Bradford told Petey to join them. Slim, Singer, and Esteban would take over in a couple of hours. Then Bradford and I would go into Laredo for supplies.

I couldn't fall asleep. Part was excitement, part the lumpy bed and the sun in the cabin window. Part was Bradford's snoring that started the minute his body hit the bunk, the knapsack with his new boots wedged beneath his head. But most of it was dead men. I couldn't move the rustlers from the space before my eyes. The muscled one who had a fury in his brow, the short one who was crying.

Thinking about dead men took me back to Missouri to when I was a boy, made me remember what I didn't want to. I tried to conjure up the image of Amelia, so she could soothe my soul and sail me into sleep. I tried to call up that

sweet, sweet face, first the easy trying I was used to, and
then I bent to the effort with a purpose that made my jaws
ache. After that I just curled up blinking in a hell hole of
a cabin in the middle of a sun-washed Texas nowhere, telling myself I'd no reason to be afraid.

But I was afraid. For the first time since I'd left Missouri,
I couldn't see Amelia's face, couldn't bring it up from the
deep, safe place inside me. I didn't know what that meant.
I figured it wasn't anything good, and the answer would
come when I least expected, the way such answers do.

It didn't make me feel better to think this, and so I
pushed it out of my mind and let in Bradford's snoring. In
a bit I caught the rhythm and rode on its mournful beat.
The cattle made soft, low sounds like a grown man crying,
and the next thing Halifax was shaking my shoulder and
the sun was in my eyes.

Bradford was already up. I could've used a bath, but I
settled for splashing my face and underarms with canteen
water and drying off on my shirt.

When I went outside, Bradford had gotten the cowhands
together. They'd spent half the night in Laredo, and it
showed. They looked like stragglers in an army that had
just lost another war. He asked if any of them could cook,
and a bantamlike man with a shock of red hair offered that
he could. He said he'd been a cook all his life, had worked
on a ranch and had been on more drives than he could
remember. No one got a bellyache from his food. The secret
of his success, he said, was in the seasoning: pepper was
known to settle the gut. And he had his own chuckwagon,
which would cut down on our expense because he'd rent
the wagon to us for a pittance. His name was Seth, and
Bradford told him to come stand by him, and he did, looking pleased and important.

While I watched, Bradford circled the rest of the men

like he would a herd, and cut out three who stood rubbing their faces. The others he dismissed with a wave of his hand and they slouched back to the lean-tos they'd slept in. If they were disappointed at not being chosen for back-breaking work, there was nothing about them that showed it.

Bradford told the men he was trail boss, that the two thousand eleven head beyond the camp were the cows we'd drive to Kansas. He told them the pay was thirty dollars a month with a five-dollar bonus per man if we lost less than fifty head. He said he was fair but took no guff. He believed in an honest day's work for a day's wage, and as long as that happened, no one would have problems with him.

The sun was bright and the sky clear blue, and Bradford paced like a general, and he'd put his new boots on. I thought his speech was pretty good, but the newly hired hands stood with all the passion of just grazed and watered cattle.

Bradford called me over and introduced me as the drover, the man who, with his brothers, owned the herd. I went from cowboy to cowboy, I shook each hand, and looked each in the face. Simon needed a shave. Marlon's blue eyes made me squint. Wyatt had a nose that had been broken and hands the size of hams. All of them squinted at me as if I was some critter they'd never laid eyes on, and nodded like I'd said, "This is Monday." I wondered if it was because I was colored, but something told me it wasn't.

Bradford told the men that him and me were going into Laredo to get supplies. While we were gone they were to start branding the calves. Then he sent Singer to fetch Petey and Esteban so they'd know everyone they'd be working with.

That's when the ugliness started.

"Mexicans?" said Wyatt. "We got to work with Mexicans?"

"No," Bradford said. "You can go where the hell you want."

"Mexicans ain't Americans," Wyatt said, and spit.

"They smell funny," Simon said. "They take jobs for less money than us."

I looked at Petey and Esteban. They were looking off into the distance as if they didn't understand. The lines above Bradford's eyes were touching. "Everybody makes the same," he said.

"I ain't cooking no Mexican food," Seth said. "They eat what the rest of us do."

"Listen hard to me," Bradford said, and I'd never heard his voice like that. "These men are going with us. They'll be paid the same, work the same, eat the same. You got a problem, state it now, and someone will take your place."

Inside, I was shaking my head. I'd thought I'd run into sticky times over a colored man being a drover. I thought some whites might resent it, and want to know how I'd come into money to buy two thousand head. But I didn't expect problems like this.

I waited, wondering if anyone would take Bradford up on his challenge. When nobody did, he told them to start building the chute and the fires, and I told Grafton that the brand was in my saddlebag beneath where I'd slept. The men shuffled off to do Bradford's bidding. Him and me saddled up and headed to town with Seth.

We took the same route we'd taken to get out to Chester's, Seth driving the wagon. We went back across tan land strewn with cactus that wore white and yellow flowers. The heat was a room without door or windows, and the butte that soared to the sky like a totem was exactly where we'd left it.

In a little while I could see the edge of Laredo, the clapboard houses, the graveyard, and the bridge in the sunlight. I remember thinking that it was less than two days since we'd left Laredo for Chester's and how strange it was that the first trip to somewhere took longer than the journey back.

We hitched our horses outside the general store. I told Bradford and Seth to start buying on their own, and I went down the street to the post office.

The postmaster hadn't changed his shirt since I'd seen him, although the President didn't seem so mad. There were two letters from Amelia. I resisted the urge to read them on the spot. I put them inside my shirt, where they'd stay until I got back to camp. Then I'd find a place to read them in private.

Having those letters improved my disposition. The day didn't seem so hot. The people in the street looked friendly and familiar, and I said "Good afternoon" to everyone I passed in a voice that was maybe too loud.

When I stepped inside the general store, Bradford and Seth were dickering with the owner. I kept out of it, wandered through small aisles left by sacks of grain and flour, pots, pans, and bolts of cloth, some white, some calico. I passed feed buckets and shovels. The store had a smell I'd never smelled, a mixture of everything sold there. The mix made my stomach feel funny, so I went outside. When Bradford called to me to settle the bill, half the afternoon was gone.

The three of us loaded the wagon and headed back to Chester's. When we arrived, the men had built the chute and started the fires. I slipped off by myself to the rise that protected the camp. I sat with my back against a boulder. I held the letters to my nose, and when I found the faint scent of perfume, I smiled like I'd just made my fortune.

Then I read the letters, taking my time. When I finished, I read them again.

Amelia still loved me. All was right with the world.

I just had to make sure she never found out what I'd been part of.

That night I sat in front of a fire, writing to Amelia. I described the smell of longhorns and the vast power of the sky. I described the heat and the land that swept in all directions. I told her about the Rio Grande, the river we'd crossed to another country. I said I missed her, and I'd be home as soon as I could.

Grafton and Halifax had gone into town—Hal, I suspected, to see the lovely whore; Grafton to see any woman who'd have him. Singer, the colored boy with the banjo, wandered over to me. I invited him to sit down.

"Writing a letter?" he said.

I nodded, and he smiled. Then he just stared into the fire, still smiling. He looked retarded or contented, I couldn't say which.

"Something on your mind, Singer?"

"Well," he said, "me and the other colored cowboys wants you to know how proud you make us. People always saying Negroes can't do nothing for themselves, but you and your brothers gives that the lie. You know, buying a herd and all. Yes, sir," he repeated, "you makes us proud."

"Well, thank you, Singer," I said. "That's right kind of you."

"You welcome," he said, and stared, still smiling at something above my head.

"Will there be anything else, Singer? You being treated all right?"

"I'm treated just fine," he said, and stood. "Well, I'll be going now."

"You have a good night, Singer."

"Thank you, sir. You, too."

When he was gone, I thought about his visit. I appreciated what Singer had said, but I wished I didn't have to be seen as an exception to how colored folks were supposed to be. I wished there were hundreds of us doing what I was doing, and I believed one day there would be. The war was over. We were free, and we could do anything white people could do as long as we were given the chance.

At the same time, while I understood why Singer felt proud, he also made me consider the difference between how others saw me and how I saw myself. People looked at me and saw "colored." I looked at me and saw "man." Not that I had to be reminded that I was colored, it just struck me how seldom I thought of myself that way. I might think from time to time about how the things I was trying to do were extra tough for my kind, but I didn't wake up in the morning and say "Good-morning, Mr. Negro." I woke up thankful for being alive. When I looked at a sunset, or stared at the dawn, I didn't think about being a colored man moved by beauty, just that I was a man who was. Most of the time I thought about being colored only when somebody, generally white, acted in a way that made me remember, and usually the way they acted was meant to make me feel bad. When that happened, it just gave me more reason to be proud of what I was, despite what my country thought of us.

Still, it was more complicated than that, and I decided to write Amelia about what my little talk with Singer had made me feel. Sometimes writing helped me make things clear to myself.

Bradford came over, grunted in greeting, then sat. For a

moment I resented the interruption, but then I thought I could write a letter anytime, so I relaxed and stared with him into the fire. The silence was comfortable, and the flames leaped and spit, and when I looked beyond the camp, I saw the horizon's deep blue lines. There was something fine about being in a wide-open space in front of a fire with a companion who didn't need to talk.

Just as I thought this, Bradford said, "Branding be done by evening two days from now. We can head north the day after that."

"Good," I said. "I'm ready."

He looked at the paper in my hand. He looked away. He looked at the paper again. "Where'd you learn to write?"

"A little school back in Missouri. Run by the parents of the woman I love."

"That's who you writing to? Your woman?"

I nodded.

"I'd like to be able to write," he said. "One day, when I got the time, I'm going to learn."

"It's a good thing to know."

"And read," he said. "I can read a little, but I want to read real good. Makes a man feel like he's somebody when he can read."

"It does."

For a while, we watched the dancing fire.

Bradford said, "I know you didn't shoot those rustlers last night. I saw you aim above their heads."

I sat, thinking of what he'd said. He hadn't asked me a question, so I didn't answer.

"Country we going through is hard, dangerous. Man needs to know he can count on who he rides with."

"Those men were unarmed," I said. "They were hardly dangerous."

"They were rustlers," Bradford said. "Range law says rustlers die."

"Well," I said, "then the law was kept."

"You got a thing about killing," Bradford said. "Ain't nothing wrong with that. But men you ride with need to know you'll be there if they need you."

He paused, and I thought, *He told me that already.* But I didn't say it. I just grunted to let him know I was listening.

He said, "Sometimes you ain't got time to make up your mind about what's right. Sometimes you have to do and figure later."

He was going on too long. He wasn't learning me nothing I didn't know. I had two choices. I could tell him to back off, that I was a man like he was. Or I could try to keep the peace with someone I needed to get all those cows to Kansas.

"That's the way I look at it," I said. "I'll never be easy with killing, but you can count on me."

For awhile he sat with his head to one side as if studying what I'd said. Then he looked off to his right, and he spoke to the horizon.

"You ever done it? Killed somebody?"

I didn't skip a beat. "Yes, I have." I said it in the exact tone of voice he'd used to tell me where he'd learned to speak Spanish.

The fire leapt and kept the darkness beyond the space we sat in. For a moment it felt like him and me were the only two folks in the world. Then he stood.

"See you later," he said, and moved off into the night.

CHAPTER SIX

I sat awhile, and the moon came out. It was round and fat and stared down at me like a disapproving eye. I scowled back at it. Bradford had made me mad. I knew the world was armed and dangerous, and I didn't take lightly to someone thinking he had to remind me. I also didn't care for his suggestion that the measure of a man was in being able to kill. But what did I expect from a man who couldn't read and write?

The minute I thought that, I knew I wasn't being fair. Chances are Bradford hadn't been taught because learning to read was against the law for colored folks wherever he'd grown up. And I had to admit that sometimes even I saw my attitude toward killing as weakness.

I also knew nobody was perfect, and that every man had something he chose not to share with others. Bradford had a mother who spoke Spanish, and I hadn't pushed him to discuss it when it was clear he didn't want to. I stayed out of his business. So why didn't he stay out of mine? You didn't have to know how to read to understand that.

I was stewing, thinking how stupid it was that men killed so easy, and the rustlers rose before my eyes. Before I could stop it, I was deep in the feeling that had visited me twice in three days, the sickness in the stomach, the red wall building behind my eyes. I swallowed and tried to cut off the feeling, but the memory was on me, and I was reliving what had happened that had made me the way I was.

It was summer in Missouri, a July day that didn't want to end. I was sixteen, and restless. I'd spent the morning doing my chores and hanging around the house, until my mama told me to get out from under her feet. Halifax and Grafton were off at a neighboring farm, having spent the night with a friend's family. I thought about saddling my horse and riding into Highland Fields, the nearest town, just to see what was happening on the streets. Highland Fields was about forty-five minutes away. But the more I thought about going, the less I wanted to do it.

I decided to go look for Caesar. Maybe he'd be in the mood to tell a story. Maybe we'd go hunting, or head down to the stream and fish for perch.

Of course, I could have gone hunting or fishing by myself. But I was having a hard time being with myself, and I was too young to know that sometimes that feeling is normal.

I found Caesar out behind the barn. Caesar's the oldest person I know. He wears his gray-streaked hair cut so close you can see his scalp. A large bronze medallion on a leather thong hangs around his neck. The medallion is so old it has no features. When I asked him what it was he said he didn't know. A Comanche brave had given it to him with the promise that it would ward off evil. The Comanche didn't say where the medallion had come from.

If Caesar had any family of his own, he never mentioned them. When he arrived, looking for work and a place to live out his days in dignity, my mother hired him, and he'd been a part of our family ever since. Me and my brothers knew how to ride and shoot when he came, but Caesar made us better. He taught us to move silently through the woods, which plants were safe to eat if we were stranded, which ones were poison. We learned how the moon and stars could mark our way at night, and how the next day's weather was in the wind. And he told us stories about the wilderness that my daddy had loved.

Caesar was sitting on the ground when I found him, leaning against the barn's north wall. In front of him was a stack of clothes, and he was darning a hole in a pair of red long underwear. My mama had offered to do this for him, but he'd always politely refused. My mama never quite forgave Caesar. She said mending was woman's work. She said it in a way that sounded like Caesar was denying her something that was her right.

"Hi, Caesar," I said. "What you doing?"

He looked up.

"Who are you?" he asked.

I laughed. "Caesar, you know who I am."

"And you know what I'm doing."

"Oh," I said.

"You're bored." His eyes were fixed on his mending. "So you ask a dumb question. Being bored will make you do that. Ain't no excuse for a man to be bored. Means he's got no purpose. No imagination. Whenever you get bored, check yourself."

I said I understood, but I didn't. I tried to get him into a conversation. I tried about six different topics, including women, who I had an abiding curiosity about, and an ignorance deeper than a river.

Caesar said, "You can stay here if you want to and watch me mend these clothes, but you got to be quiet. I ain't in no mood for talking. Neither are you. You just want something to do. And it ain't me you want to do it with.''

I looked away so he wouldn't see that he'd hurt my feelings. I told him I'd see him later. He grunted. I went back inside the house and my mama said, "I thought I told you to go outside," and I said I'd come for my rifle, a Remington .22, a present for my fourteenth birthday. I grabbed two boxes of shells and strolled out to the field where Caesar had set up a shooting range, and I stood blasting away at the targets. At sixteen I was a crack shot, thanks both to Caesar's teaching and to what he allowed was natural talent. He said a rifle seemed a part of me, and I knew what he meant; when I aimed at something it was as if my whole body was pointing, and most targets too big to miss. For me a bad shot was two inches outside a bull's-eye the size of a fist clenched at fifty paces.

In a little I started shooting on the move, standing with my back to the target, whirling to fire in one motion. Then I'd run ten steps to the right, fall to the ground, roll, come to my knees. I remember how the sky spun a rich man's blue, and how the trees looked like soldiers guarding the fallow field. I remember how I didn't miss.

After I got through telling myself how good I was, the boredom came down again. It was like itching all over my body, and emptiness in my gut, and it didn't help that Caesar had said the boredom was because of a lack in me.

I tried to figure out what I wanted to do, and the only thing I could come up with was the urge for a moving target, to shoot at something alive. So I cut back across in front of the house and headed for the woods.

The woods were cool and deep, and I moved sure and quiet, the way Caesar had taught me. I sniffed the hot, thick afternoon, identified the smell of oak and elm and birch, fir and spruce. Here and there were blazes of wood flowers growing in soil kept damp by tree shade. A couple of times, startled by my presence, a bird shot out of a tree, spiraled frantically toward the sky. Once I had a crow the size of a hawk in my sights, its feathers so black the sun made them purple, but I didn't shoot. Chipmunks stood on hind legs, staring at me with hard, bright eyes, and from the branches above, squirrels scurried and called me everything but a child of God. I saw a woodchuck as big as a puppy, and I could have bagged it, but I didn't. Everything—the birds, the squirrels and chipmunks, the woodchuck—were all too easy prey, fit maybe for a beginner, but not a first-rate shot like me. I wanted a challenge, and I'd wait until I found one.

I plunged deeper into the woods, forded the brook from rock to slippery rock. The moss was a green so deep it was quiet. Minnows flashed in the icy water, and I could see all the way to the bottom. Through gaps in the treetops two shafts of sunlight dropped straight down from the sky. The shafts were shaped like the flat boards the barn was built from. They were maybe four feet apart. They carved through shadow, dove into the brook and made it shimmer. At the base of each shaft, insects massed and darted, as if discussing light's origins and whether they'd fly up to find it.

Something buzzed near my ear. I slapped at it and looked at my hand. I flicked away the bloody remains of a mosquito who'd staked out my neck for lunch, then looked back the way I'd come. I could feel my boredom growing like something angry and alive, massing like the insects, moving furiously, going nowhere.

Caesar had said I had no imagination. But I did, and I proved it to him by making up a dream.

I was scouting for a wagon train. I'd gone ahead to negotiate with the Indians for passage through their land. I spoke Indian as if born to it, and the chief, a hard little man with muscles like knots and eyes that had no bottoms, had said okay. It should have been easy after that, just get back to the wagons, and lead them through. But some of the young braves had decided not to let settlers spoil their rivers and shoot their game, and so, without telling the chief, a bunch of them had trailed me. They planned to kill me before I got back to the train, then they'd set upon the settlers and scalp the men and children and rape the women.

I knew this because I was careful. Being careful was how I'd earned my reputation as the best damn scout in the territory. I'd doubled back and heard the young braves plotting, and one of them had seen me, and without so much as a word, they'd moved out to get my hide. Now they had me trapped, and I knew I was a goner, but I also knew that I'd take some of them with me, or my name wasn't Joshua Partlow.

And when I thought this, I heard something heavy moving on my left. All the ruckus should have told me it wasn't an Indian, no self-respecting Indian would have made all that noise. But my life was in danger, and I didn't have time to think. I spun and rolled, came up behind a tree that gave me a little protection, and I caught the movement, saw a flash of white and brown, and I was firing into its center.

The rifle crack brought me out of my dreaming, slammed me hard against the knowing that what I'd just done was about as dumb as I could get. I'd probably shot a deer, which meant I'd have the back-breaking job of gutting it and hauling it back to the farm. Or if my luck was really bad, I'd shot a stray calf belonging to a neighbor. Annoyed with myself, I got up, moved forward toward the brush that hid my target, parted the branches.

I felt the hole open in my stomach. For the first time in my life, the red wall rose behind my eyes. I didn't have-enough air to breathe, and I remember thinking that if I didn't control it, my fear would kill me.

I'd shot a boy, a white boy no older than myself. The hole in his throat was gushing. He looked like a drifter. Stringy blond hair fell across his forehead, and his clothes were worn and dirty, and he had that look that said he'd been missing meals.

I was swallowing hard to keep what was happening in my stomach from coming to my mouth, but I couldn't stop it, and I turned and puked. Then, my head swimming so hard the sky turned, I prayed for a miracle. I went to my knees, picked up the dirty hand. It was warm and heavy. I put two fingers on the wrist.

It was the deepest silence I'd ever known, deeper than sleep or the center of the woods in winter, and I knew that if I didn't watch out I'd fall into it forever.

I stood up, shaking. The only person who could help me now was Caesar.

I found Caesar where I'd left him, head bowed above his mending. I told him what had happened and he listened without comment. He could have said how he'd taught me never to fire unless I was sure of what I aimed at. He could have said that not more than an hour had passed since he'd warned me about being bored.

"You sure he's dead?"

When I nodded, sickened, he stood, went into the barn, came back with a shovel. "Let's go," he said, and I led him back through the woods and the chattering squirrels, across the brook with those columns of sunlight, and then we came to the body. Caesar squatted, checked the pulse. He went through the dead boy's pockets. They were as empty as the space in me.

"Over there," Caesar said.

"What?"

"Over there. Drag the body over there."

"Why?"

"Shut up," he said, without raising his voice. "Shut up and do what I tell you."

I bent, grabbed the body under the shoulders, dragged it the twenty feet to where he'd pointed, between two birch trees so white and slender they didn't look real. When I turned, Caesar had started digging. He worked in silence, and I stood, careful not to look at the body. I looked at the patches of blue sky visible through the treetops. I looked at the tiny wildflowers whose name I couldn't recall. They were blue and yellow, and they grew where the sunlight fell. Then I couldn't look at anything, and I shut my eyes and waited for whatever it was that would happen.

"Hey," Caesar said.

I opened my eyes. The hole was about six feet long, three wide and three deep, and he climbed out of it, handed me the shovel. "Get in," he said. "Dig till I tell you to stop."

The ground wasn't all that hard, but it was work, and I'd begun to feel the muscles ache in the back of my shoulders when Caesar said, "That's enough."

He reached down and helped me out of the hole I'd dug. We rolled the boy into the gaping grave. We covered the body and stomped the dirt. We took branches and swept the ground. Then we stopped, and I heard our breathing.

All this time I had the feeling that Caesar hadn't looked at me. Now he did. "You don't need me to tell you what you did wrong," he said. "But you might need me to tell you we just broke the law."

He was looking straight into my eyes, holding them, and I wanted to drop my eyes, but I knew he'd insist that I didn't. He didn't look or sound angry, just intense.

"You ain't never to tell this to no one. Not your mama,

your brothers, or your wife if you ever get one. You understand?"

I said I did.

"Be times when you need to tell. When the feeling comes if you tell, then all's forgiven."

He took a deep breath, let it out. "Don't trust that feeling. Take a long walk or a drink or find a woman. But don't give in to it. You understand?"

I said I did.

"It was an accident," Caesar said. "A dumb, fool accident, but that's what it is. You got to live with it, but you ain't got to die from it. You see what I'm saying?"

I nodded.

"Let's get out of here," he said. "It's finished."

But it wasn't finished. I lived with it. It drove me out into the fields where day after day I practiced with the single-mindedness of a madman developing my ability to shoot to wound rather than kill. It was years before I stopped looking over my shoulder for the lawman who'd come to arrest me. Maybe it wouldn't have been so bad if I hadn't fallen in love with Amelia and if she hadn't said to me that she could never love a man who could take another's life. Maybe it would have been better if I'd told Amelia at the beginning. She might have understood.

But I remembered what Caesar had said, and I didn't tell her. I didn't tell her because not only had I taken a life, I'd hidden it. Even if she'd forgiven me for the first, she wouldn't have for the second. For me the hiding of it didn't seem all that important until later. Then I learned hiding was worst of all.

The funny part was I thought some of why Amelia was drawn to me had to do with my outlook on killing. I'd told her I could never do it, and she made it more than a feeling in common, she made it a bond. But my feelings weren't natural like she thought they were. I was a convert to the faith of not-killing, a zealot who'd never confessed, who kept his sin a secret.

I'd gone to church enough to know you couldn't be saved without repentance. But as I grew older, I put that knowing on a shelf in the back of my mind. I placed it there with all the resignation of a man who's hiding something he knows he'll one day have to tell to a hanging judge.

It wasn't easy to carry all of that around, and as the years passed, I worked real hard at forgetting. But now I'd come to Texas, a place where men took one another's lives in the way I swatted mosquitoes. The fact was that no matter how hard I tried not to, the chance was that someday, before I got back to Missouri, I'd end up killing someone, or end up dead if I couldn't. In either case, I'd lose Amelia and never get to Montana.

Forgetting wasn't easy in the presence of these facts.

CHAPTER SEVEN

Over the next two days, working from dawn to dusk, we did the branding. The air was sharp with the smell of burned hide and hair. Some of the cattle flinched at the branding iron, some paid it no mind, and most let out a bellow. These mournful sounds filled my dreams at night. They sang in my head during waking like a two-note funeral song.

Once I saw Grafton and Halifax talking to one another, serious-like, and Halifax said something angry, and Grafton shook his head and walked away. After that I kept an eye out. I didn't want anything coming between my brothers on our four-month journey north.

My watching led me to believe that Grafton seemed okay. He was his easygoing, joking self. It was Halifax who wasn't right. He acted like he had something on his mind, something so heavy even hard work couldn't distract him. When I asked, he said he was fine. I didn't believe him. But if a man doesn't want you in his business, you back off and leave him alone.

The branding was finished about four o'clock. The cowhands, including my brothers, were going into town for one last chance at carousing. Bradford told everybody to be back by midnight, so that we could head out at the crack of dawn. Anybody who hadn't gotten his required sleep or who'd drunk too much and couldn't pull his load would be fired on the spot.

Before he left for town, Grafton came over to where I sat in the door of the cabin. He was dressed for a party. He'd washed his face and hands and beat the dust from his clothes, and wore a red bandanna. I told him he looked right nice, but he didn't smile.

"We got a problem," he said. He was looking out over the backs of longhorns, away from the setting sun.

"What kind of problem?"

"Halifax wants to take the whore with him."

"You're pulling my leg."

"Wish I was. Fallen for her hook, line, and sinker. Been with her the last two nights."

"He can't take her with him," I said. "That's just his nature talking. What's it going to look like, him with a whore for a woman? How's she going to survive a cattle drive? What's Mama going to say?"

"Maybe he'll listen to you," Grafton said. He stood, rolled his head as if his neck had a crick in it.

"Oh," he said. "When you talk to him, don't call her a whore. He'll get besides himself."

I found Halifax over at the corral, brushing down his horse. When he saw me, he started to smile, but then, as if he knew why I was there, his face shut down. He began to brush the horse with a force that would have taken the skin off an animal less tough.

"Hey," I said. "You ready for the morning?"

He nodded.

"Grafton said you got something on your mind."

"Grafton talks more than he needs to."

I hesitated, and then I jumped right in. "It ain't a good idea, brother. A cattle drive's no place for a woman."

I counted the number of times he brushed that horse before he spoke, six.

"Excuse me," he said, "but ain't you in my business?"

"A little," I said. "On the other hand, we're trying to move two thousand head of cattle to Kansas. It ain't going to be no picnic. Anything makes it harder—that's everybody's business."

His face looked like he was in pain.

"She can make it," he said. "She's as strong as some men I know. She don't look it, but she is. And she can ride with the cook. There's room on the wagon."

"Hal. You haven't thought this through. It doesn't make sense."

"Why don't you just come out with what you're thinking?" he said. His teeth were clenched. He was brushing that horse like there was no tomorrow, and a muscle jumped in his jaw.

I tried to keep my voice even. "Listen, you ain't the first man to feel what you feel. It'll pass, believe me."

"You speaking from experience?"

"Not exactly."

"Then the best you can do is guess what I feel. Or how I feel it."

"I'm just saying it'll pass."

"And if I don't want it to pass?"

I shrugged. "It will, anyway."

Halifax shook his head. "I'm surprised at you, big brother. Don't have the stomach to say what you really think: What will folks say if Halifax comes home with a whore?" His voice had risen. By the time he'd finished, it was a shout.

"I didn't say that."

"I'm not talking about what you said. I'm talking about what you thinking."

"Halifax. . . ."

"You made up your mind because of what somebody does for a living." He'd stopped brushing the horse. He was facing me, his eyes were deadly, and his empty hand was a fist. "You don't know why she does it. Things happen to people. They end up doing things they wouldn't have done if circumstance was different. Our daddy was a slave. Our mama, too. Remember?"

"I understand that," I said. "I only want what's best for you. I want you to do what makes you happy in the long run. That's all I'm saying. Think about why we're here, what we hope to accomplish. That's all."

He didn't answer. Then I had an idea so bright it made me blink. "Listen, what's to stop you coming back to get her after the drive is done?"

"I thought of that. But I can't stand the thought of what would be happening while I'm gone."

"Halifax, I can't let you do it."

For a moment I thought he might take a swing at me.

" 'Cause you older than me don't mean I ain't a man," he said. "Quiet as it's kept, you can't keep me from doing nothing. I ain't got to go with you. You and Grafton can go on by yourself."

"We're in this together. We're brothers, remember? And we promised to do this together."

He was inspecting the horse's fetlocks, bent over in front of me, face hidden. "That's the thing about promises," he said. "They's all the time getting broken."

"This one don't have to be."

"You just don't understand," he said, and a weary was in his voice.

"Maybe not. There could be something here I'm missing. Something complicated, deep. But I do know it'll kill your mama.''

He flinched when I said that, stood and stared at me, and I stared back, knowing I was playing dirty, but knowing he'd left me no choice.

''Mama ain't dying no time soon.''

''She will if she hears about what you plan to do.''

He didn't answer.

''Leave the . . . woman here, Hal. Come back for her if you want. Break your mama's heart. But do it after we move these cattle.''

He stood, still looking at me, and I wondered if I'd over-played my hand by crowding him into a corner. Hal didn't like tight places, never even liked being indoors too much. When he was a kid, and the weather let him, he'd pitch a tent rather than sleep in his bed. In the winter he was always stepping outside for what he said was air.

I didn't realize it till later, but I was holding my breath, wondering how'd he react. He might go off with the whore out of retaliation now, do something else that was crazy.

I kept staring at him, hoping I hadn't lost his respect, hoping he'd understand later that I'd done what I had to do.

''Halifax,'' I said. ''What's it to be?''

He'd turned his back to me, stared off into the distance. He was shaking his head. I hoped it didn't mean ''no.'' I hoped it wasn't in disbelief at the depths I'd sunk to get him to change his mind.

''Don't worry,'' he said, and his voice was flat. ''I'll be ready in the morning. Alone.''

Relief sat down inside me. I said to have a good time his last night in town. Then I walked back to the cabin, spun, saddled up my horse, rode out of camp for a quarter of an hour, then stopped and started shooting. I shot at a rock the size of a fist, the bump on a log that was rotting. I blew the head off a lizard minding nobody's business but his own. I kept firing, blasted the flowers that grew at the feet of some brush. I was trying to make the empty inside me go away, but it wouldn't. It hung with me while I ate and cared for my horse and tried to write another letter to Amelia. I didn't feel like writing. I walked up to the ridge and looked out over the sea of cattle. I imagined walking on their backs toward the horizon. I went searching for Bradford but couldn't find him. Finally, I stretched out on that lumpy cot and slept.

I dreamed of a flat, dark land and a space between me and Amelia. Voices started up in the dream. One said that if I jumped across the space, I could fly to my true love's arms. The other said that if I tried, I'd fall to my destruction. I listened to the first voice, took the risk, and found I couldn't fly. I was dropping toward an unseen bottom where strange beasts snarled a promise to eat me. Amelia was calling as I fell, and I reached toward her. The wind roared in my ears, and the beasts below me were longhorns, and Grafton was shaking me and saying Halifax was in jail.

I remember the first thing I felt was relief that the dream wasn't real. Then it sunk in what Grafton had said, and I was watching myself being calm.

I glanced to my right. Bradford was in his bunk, snoring, head turned toward the wall.

"What happened?" I asked.

"He'd planned to pay to spend the night with her, but when he got there, she was with somebody else. A white man. When he came out, somebody said something to him about Halifax having feelings for the girl, and the cowboy said something to Halifax. Next thing I know they's having words, and reaching for their guns."

Grafton sighed. "It was a fair fight. But Hal was beside himself and when the cowboy turned the first time Hal shot him, Hal put a couple more bullets in his back. When they called the sheriff, he looked at the holes in the cowboy's back and arrested Hal. Everybody tried to tell him what happened, but he wouldn't hear it. Said he was tired of colored cowboys shooting up his town. Said he was holding Hal till the judge comes through a couple of weeks from now."

I felt sick to my stomach. "Bradford," I called.

He came awake quick, rolled from the bunk in one motion. I told him what Grafton had told me.

He rubbed a hand over his face. He looked at the ceiling and scratched his head with both hands. "Okay," he said. "We keep to our plans. Move out in the morning."

"What about my brother?" I said.

"We head out like we're leaving him. We double back in a couple of days and bust him out of jail."

It took a moment for what he said to make sense. "That's against the law," I said.

"You got a better idea?" He was hot with me. "You want law or you want justice? You ain't lived long enough to know the difference?"

I looked at him. I remember thinking how strange it was that the world had produced us both. At the same time, I was confused. The idea of a jailbreak was as unreal as the unthinking part of me that accepted it. I knew something was going on in me that needed figuring out, but I'd have to do it later.

"Okay," I said. "But I'm going to see him before we leave. No way I want him thinking we just up and left him. I'll be at the jail by first light."

Bradford said, "I'd planned to leave at dawn. But I'll give you two hours after that. Be here."

I looked at him. I started to remind him that I was the boss, but I didn't.

"And be careful," he said. "Keep your voice down. Don't do nothing to rile no one. I don't want to have to break two of you out of jail."

Grafton said, "Shouldn't I go with him?"

"Better if he goes alone," Bradford said. "Don't want to make nobody nervous, thinking we're up to something." He looked at me. "Get a good look at the jail. Doors, strength of walls, that sort of thing. The lay of the land out back."

He sat down on his bunk, stretched and fell backward as if felled with an ax. He was snoring before his head hit the bag that he kept his new boots in.

Grafton was watching me. He was worried. I told him everything would be all right. I wasn't so sure, but it was my job to say it. He nodded and said he'd see me in the morning. The last thing he said before he left was, "Be careful."

I stretched out on the lumpy bed, but it was impossible to sleep.

When the gray started to crawl across the sky, dragging the promise of morning, I swung from my bunk, saddled my horse, and rode toward Laredo. I felt on a first-name basis with the journey, nodded to the butte and the mesas. At the edge of town, the cemetery looked peaceful, and the smoke came from the houses.

Only a few people moved on the street, stragglers going home or wherever after a night of drinking and gambling or the sweet forgetting of a young whore's willing flesh. I wondered if any of the men had wives and how they'd explain where they'd come from.

I tied my horse in front of the jailhouse and went inside.

The sheriff wasn't around, but his deputy was—a tall man with dark hair and a pinched face. He slept on a chair, his feet in boots that reminded me of the ones Bradford had worn when I met him. The deputy smiled in his sleep and said something low. I wondered what he was dreaming, and if he'd remember it when he awoke.

The room was small, with two desks and a front window. The cells were at the back. Guarding the entrance to the cells was a heavy door with a metal plate around the keyhole. The door had a small barred opening at the top, and while I could see through to part of a cell, I couldn't see if anyone was in it.

I cleared my throat and the deputy came awake with a start, standing up with the expression of a man caught in the act of stealing. When he saw it was me, his eyebrows raised. I told him I was here to see my brother.

"Kind of early, ain't you?"

I started to tell him that I hadn't seen any visiting hours posted on the door, but I remembered what Bradford had said about not riling anyone. I just nodded.

The deputy held his hand out.

"Your weapon," he said.

I unbuckled my belt, handed it to him. He hung it on a hook on a wall. Then he came toward me.

"Turn around," he said. "Hands out."

He patted me down. I didn't like the feel of his hands on my body. I think he liked the excuse to touch me. His breath was foul, and he needed a bath.

When he was finished, he reached for the ring of keys on the desk. He put one in the heavy door and turned it. I heard the click of an opening lock, and the door swung slow toward me. The deputy stepped back, then motioned me to go forward, and I breathed deep and stepped inside.

There were three cells. Halifax was in the one to my

right, sitting on the bunk with his head in his hands. He looked thin and miserable. The door closed behind me, and I walked toward my brother.

"How you doing?" I asked.

He shrugged. He moved his foot through the bars of morning light that stole through the cell's one window.

"They ain't mistreating you?"

He shook his head.

"Josh, you got to get me out of here. You know I can't stand being cooped up."

"I know."

"He drew on me first."

He said it with the tone of a man who'd been dying to tell his story, but had only now found someone to believe it. "I'm just standing there, telling him I wasn't going to take his guff, and he reached for his gun, Josh. . . ."

He was talking in a rush, his eyes begging me for things I couldn't give him.

"Hush," I whispered. "Grafton told me what happened. He saw it all."

"You got to get me out of here."

"I will, but you have to be patient. We'll get you out, but we can't do it right this minute."

I told him about the plan. He looked a little doubtful.

"That's breaking the law. And we're colored men in Texas."

"I know that, but it's the only way. You got to be strong and trust me."

I looked at him straight, but I wasn't nearly as sure as I sounded.

He sniffed. "How long I got to stay here?"

"A couple of days. Maybe four at the most."

"Four *days*?"

"Keep your voice down," I said.

"What if something happens to you, what if . . ."

I made my voice hard. "Ain't nothing going to happen to me. And you got to play your part. Behave yourself. Keep calm, have faith. Have I ever let you down?"

He shook his head, but still he didn't like it.

"Come over here," I said.

He got up from the bunk and came toward me. I reached through the bars and held his arms.

"You're my brother," I said.

He put his arms through the bars. He had his hands on my shoulders.

"It's going to be all right," I promised. "I got to go now. Be strong."

I felt his hands tighten. I could feel them when the deputy returned my gun and watched while I strapped it on. I could feel them when I went outside and walked to the back of the jail. Nothing was behind the jail except open space. I checked the walls. They were a foot and a half thick, but the places where the bars were set were crumbling. A man on a horse could put a rope around those bars and pull them out with no trouble. But that ought not to be necessary. If we came for Halifax in the night, and only one or two men were guarding the jail, we could walk him out the front door.

I don't remember the ride back to Chester's. My horse knew the way by now, and I let him have his head as we rode toward the rising sun.

When I got back to camp, I told Grafton and Bradford what had happened. Grafton looked worried, and I told him not to be, that somehow things would work out.

Bradford said it was time to get going. We had a herd to move, and half the morning was gone.

Part
TWO

CHAPTER EIGHT

By the time the sun was blazing, Bradford let out a shout and we started the long drive north to Kansas. The cattle were rested and fed and seemed eager to make the journey. If Halifax had been with us, it would have been perfect. I bent my mind to moving those cows and let the work distract me. When I rode to the top of a bluff, the line of cows stretched for more than a mile. I could see how the hands worked to keep the proper spacing, so the trailing cattle wouldn't walk dumbly up the backs of the ones in front. First came Bradford, and Marlon, the boy with bright blue eyes. They were the point riders. Behind them the longhorns came two by plodding two, like a slowly widening stream, the click of horns as they bumped one another like the beat of castanets. Where the cattle spread to six across rode two more cowboys, one on either side. These were called "swingers," and it was their job to keep the herd from bunching.

Several hundred feet down the line from the swingers were another two riders. At that point the cattle were allowed to bunch, and they widened to ten across.

Past the bunching, another hundred feet or so, a couple

of cowboys brought up the rear of the herd, their noses and mouths covered by bandannas to keep out the thick clouds of dust. Behind them was Seth, driving the chuckwagon. Finally, came the horses, cared for by Singer, the pudgy colored boy with the banjo who'd told me I'd made him proud. Singer was called the "wrangler," and the horses the "remuda." Besides caring for the horses, Singer would fetch water and wood or cow chips for the cook to build his fires.

Late that first afternoon, Seth swung the wagon out around the herd and talked a moment to Bradford. Then Seth went ahead to find a place suitable for camping for the night.

I saw him again an hour and a half later. He'd unhitched his horse. The wagon's tongue was pointed in the direction we'd be headed in the morning, due north, four months away from our Kansas destination.

Like I said, the work had distracted me a little. Now, at the end of the day, Halifax came back to my mind. The men seemed subdued while they ate. They'd only known my brother a couple of days or so, but Caesar had told me that bonds form quickly when men come together for a purpose. I knew that a couple of cowhands had gone privately to Bradford to say we ought to delay our departure until the judge came through. They wanted somebody who knew Halifax to be there to tell his side of the story. Bradford said no. The judge wasn't due for two weeks. Two weeks meant that we could be one hundred fifty miles or so along the trail. Any judge worth his salt, given all the eyewitnesses, would free Halifax in a minute, and give the sheriff a piece of his mind about holding an innocent man. And then Halifax could ride out to meet us. It wouldn't take him long. A man on horseback could cover in a day maybe five or six times the distance that we could.

I wanted to agree with Bradford. But what if the judge *wasn't* worth his salt? What if he'd had a hard journey in and felt the need to take it out on someone? What if he was just flat-out nigger-hating, like Steele, and had a problem with coloreds shooting white folks, no matter how fair the fight?

I tried to push those thoughts out of my mind, cursing my habit of always taking into account that things might turn out for the worse. Now Bradford's plan made a lot more sense to me than it had last night. The truth was I couldn't take the chance of delivering Halifax into the unknown hands of Texas justice. I'd no way of knowing if it was blind. And if it wasn't, then my brother could end up being hanged for something he hadn't done. I didn't like any of it, including breaking the law. I'd promised myself that the first time I'd broken the law would be the last. But if it came to that, or giving up my brother's life, I knew what I'd do. And I'd adjust to it. I didn't make this world, but I had to live in it.

That first day we got in eight miles before night fell, and the next we made thirteen. Nothing out of the ordinary happened except that one of the horses got bit by a rattlesnake and had to be destroyed. Seth said he'd save the meat for supper, and Slim said horse would be an improvement over what we'd eaten so far.

I liked being out here, sleeping in the open. I liked the easy camaraderie of the men and sitting around the fire while Singer strummed his banjo and sang. I liked the beat of cows against the trail, the click of horns, and the horses' snorts, and I even liked the smell, which was sweat and cowhide and dung. What I didn't like was the dust. It attacked my eyes, lined the roof of my mouth, found all the creases in my body. Dust collected in my nose and covered my clothes like a blanket. But even that wouldn't have bothered me if my brother had been along.

At the end of the second day I went over to Bradford, and asked when were we going for Halifax.

"Maybe tomorrow," he said.

He said the same thing at the end of the third day. I was thinking of Halifax locked up in that cell, fretting at the lack of space, wondering where was the brother who'd promised to come back for him. I was thinking of the doubt building inside him, and how tough it would be to keep his spirits up. I couldn't know if he was being treated right. Friends of the man he'd shot might right now be marching toward the jail. They'd hang him while townspeople gathered, shivering with the thrill, and the sheriff would turn his head.

That kind of thinking got me hot with Bradford. He seemed so matter of fact about when we'd go back. I wondered if he cared.

Grafton had more patience than me, and tried to calm me down, but I couldn't be calmed. I waited till after supper, when both men and cattle had settled down. Then I went looking for Bradford. As I walked around the camp, I glanced up at the sky where a million stars were shining with a quarter moon in their midst. It was grand and beautiful, and I jumped when I heard the coyote's howl. It sounded like a madman's laugh. I shivered, stopped a moment, and looked off into the darkness. I turned to go back the way I'd come and nearly stepped on something living. It scared me so bad I hollered.

It was Bradford. He was sitting on a log on the ground.

"Why you sneak up on me that way?" I sputtered.

We were away from the campfires, nothing but stars and moon to see by. His hat was hiding his face, but I had the impression he was smiling.

"Ain't sneaked up on no one," he said. "Been sitting here for close to half an hour."

I didn't believe him, but I couldn't call a man a liar without proof.

"I been looking for you."

"Well," he said, "you nearly stepped on me."

"When we going for my brother? You said a couple of days. We're up to four."

I don't know if you could call what he was doing listening to me. He sure wasn't looking at me.

"Bradford," I said.

And he said, "We're going tonight."

I felt stupid. "Tonight?"

He nodded. "Be back in Laredo before dawn. Go get some sleep. I'll wake you when it's time."

"When were you going to tell me?"

For the count of ten he looked at me like I was speaking Indian, and when he spoke it wasn't to answer my question. He said he'd wanted to give us some distance from Laredo. The farther we got away from town, the better our chances with anyone who chose to come after us. Once we came on Indian country, we ought to be safe. Ever since Steele, the Indians in this part of the country were unforgiving, and any posse would know that.

It made sense. I just didn't understand why he hadn't told me until now.

"Who's going with us?" I asked.

"Me, you, and Grafton."

I said maybe Grafton ought not to go.

"Why?"

"Well," I started, and then realized I couldn't say it. I

was thinking about Grafton's safety, didn't want anything to happen to him. But if he didn't go, someone else would have to, and I couldn't volunteer that another man should risk his life in my brother's place.

"Grafton's big, strong, and got good sense," Bradford said. "I can depend on him. Some of these others are good for driving cattle, but not much else."

"You tell Grafton?"

"Tell him what?"

I stared at him. He was being pigheaded again, playing dumb, for what reason I couldn't tell. I realized I was growing to dislike my trail boss. One day the two of us were going to have it out, but now wasn't the time.

"That we're heading out tonight."

"No. You tell him."

So I did, and Grafton just looked at me and nodded, showing none of the tension I felt.

What Bradford had said about him made me look closer. I was used to thinking of Grafton as my younger brother, someone I had to look out for. But Bradford was right. Grafton was a man, dependable, with good sense. I didn't understand why I felt like I'd lost something I'd never find again.

I tried to sleep, but the best I could manage was to doze off from time to time. After awhile I gave up and watched the star-cluttered sky. I listened to cowboys singing to the herd. I let my mind wander to my mama, to Caesar, to Amelia. Amelia's face still wouldn't come when I called. So I thought of the way her skin felt beneath my hands. I thought of the curve of her neck, and I slipped into a half-wake state where I heard her speak to me. She was reminding me that I'd promised to pray every day. I came wide awake, said the Lord's Prayer in my mind, quick-like, and when I'd finished, I felt unsatisfied, like a hungry man who dreamed of steak while he bolted a crust of bread. I swallowed hard, and then I was thinking of Steele, the man I'd humiliated in that Laredo street. Both Steele and Bradford had said I should have killed Steele, and for a moment, I wished I'd done it. Was Steele right now gathering men to come after me? Was he hidden behind the next ridge, waiting to attack?

I rolled onto my side, and held my knees to my chest. It was the best I could do for the feeling that the world was closing in. My imagination was off and running. Steele and his blood-thirsty gang, a posse hot on our trail for breaking Halifax out of jail, Indians to the north, to say nothing of all those rivers to cross. Life was going out of its way to prove how tough it could be. And there was little I could do, no large, meaningful steps I could take to prevent it. I just had to take the short steps, one foot in front of the other, doing what needed to be done at the moment need arose.

If everything turned out for the worst, then we were all in serious trouble. I consoled myself with the thought that most times life mixed the good with the bad. Maybe that's what kept all of us going, that balance, that sense that it was rare that everybody *always* ended up with the worst that could have happened.

I closed my eyes for what seemed like five seconds and Grafton was shaking me and saying it was time to go. We mounted up, and the moon and the stars lit our way. I was feeling small and strange and lonely. Me, Joshua Partlow, who obeyed the law, who'd been taught to do what was right, was going to break his brother out of jail. Who back home would believe it?

We went in a single file, Bradford first, then me, then

Grafton with a horse for our brother. No one spoke. The trail the cattle had made was clear in the light before us.

Half an hour before dawn, the lights of Laredo formed in the blue-black distance. As we came closer, shadows were everywhere, and I tried to look through them to what hid on their other sides. No smoke came from chimneys of sleeping houses, and the noise as we crossed the wooden bridge made me think we'd raise the dead.

My heart was beating in my dry and tightened throat. I could smell the sweat that pooled in my armpits. It was the cool of just before morning, and my hands on the reins were wet.

We tied our horses in front of the general store. Bradford told Grafton to stay behind, guard the mounts. He gave me a length of rope, coiled in a circle. I slipped it over my shoulder, and we moved toward the jail.

The street was deserted, but I kept expecting blinding light and buildings coming alive with voices demanding to know our business. I looked into the dark of every alley, but the night stayed black and empty.

As we approached the jail, Bradford drew his gun, kept it at his side, hidden by his thigh. I mimicked him, took a deep breath, and we walked through the front door like into our own house. By the time the deputy had come awake, Bradford had a gun at his forehead. The deputy was scared, and started to say something, but when Bradford whispered that he was a dead man if he so much as spoke, he was pleased to keep his mouth shut. I tied him to his chair, maybe a little tighter than I had to. Bradford gagged him and I took the keys that hung on the wall, opened the massive door.

I was feeling okay now, in control. My brother was standing at the window, looking, I think, at the sky. He turned to me and his face opened with relief. He didn't say anything. When I opened his cell, he came out with a walk that had purpose, but no hurry.

In the other room, Bradford was at the door, his head swiveling in all directions. He turned, waved at us to come forward. Halifax got his gun from a hook on the wall, strapped it to his waist. He tied the holster to his thigh, and smiled at me. I was thinking how easy it was, and we stepped into the morning. The sky was still black, but a ribbon of gray lined its edges.

I touched my brother's arm. I pointed toward where Grafton waited with the horses. Halifax started to go that way, then he looked at me.

"I'll be right back," he said.

"What?"

In the same moment that I understood what he'd said, he ran off in the direction of Dora's.

I was dumbfounded in the dark Laredo street.

"He's going to get us killed," Bradford hissed. He came toward me. I started to follow Halifax, and Bradford grabbed my arm.

I said, "I got to go get him."

"Don't move," Bradford said. "We'll wait a few minutes by the horses. Then we're out of here."

"I can't leave him."

"You ought to teach him some sense," Bradford said. His voice was an angry whisper. "We're risking our lives for him." He pulled me down the street toward Grafton.

Grafton said, "He's going for that whore." There was no surprise in his voice, no judgment.

Bradford was steaming. Inside my chest was a steadily tightening wire. We stood for what seemed like forever, looking back at Dora's.

"Let's go," Bradford said, and I said, "Wait," and Hal-

ifax came out of the doorway. He was holding the whore's
elbow in one hand, and had a satchel in the other. He was
pulling the whore into the street and her dress made it hard
to run. The sky shivered with early light. The buildings
were disbelieving, and Halifax and the girl came toward us
in slow and silly motion. Another figure came through the
door of Dora's, and I heard the sound of gunfire, and Halifax was spinning, firing back. The figure in the doorway
fell like his bones had turned to water. Halifax was bending
to pick up the satchel, pulling at the whore, running toward
us. I was holding my breath. I expected more shots and my
brother crumbling. I felt tight and scared and helpless, and
I thought they'd never reach us.

But they made it, and Halifax jumped onto the back of
his horse. When I boosted the lovely whore behind him, I
felt her firm flesh in my hands. I caught the scent of flowers
from soap or the perfume she wore.

Then all of us were mounted and turning to flee, down
the miracle of a still deserted street, our horses' hoofbeats
like gunshots on the bridge, and in the graveyard head-
stones glowed in the dawning. I bent low above the neck
of my gelding. I thought of nothing but putting as much
distance between me and Laredo as I could.

We rode, and the sun rose like a yellow fire, and the heat
wrapped me up like a lover refusing to go. I looked behind
me several times, but found nothing but earth and sky, the
rolling hills, a mesa dark and solemn, the dust our horses
beat.

Once I was riding neck and neck with Halifax and I
sneaked a glance at the whore. She held to Halifax's waist,
and her head was turned from me. Every time I looked at
Bradford and Grafton, I couldn't read their faces.

We rode, and came to a turn in the trail and there was
the herd, like a great brown sea before us. I was glad to

see those cattle. I was glad to see Seth scurrying to keep the coffeepot filled. My dream was still intact. I thought about how easily it could have fallen apart back in Laredo, and I felt a flush of mad at Halifax.

The men were up. They'd already eaten their beans and bread, and in a little while we'd be moving. I took one last look behind me, and we rode in a canter to meet them.

CHAPTER NINE

Bradford gathered the men and told them we'd broken Halifax out of jail. As every one could see, Bradford said, we had a woman with us. Everyone would respect her or answer to him. She'd ride on the chuckwagon with Seth and be his helper. When he asked if anybody had a question, nobody spoke.

I didn't ask my question. Why hadn't Bradford told the whole story, that my brother, in going back for the girl, had shot someone?

When I spoke to Halifax, he said he was okay. I didn't believe him, and I guess it must have been on my face.

"Josh," he said, "I'm sorry to cause so much trouble."

I shrugged. "You'd have done the same for me," I said. I tried to say it straight, but I couldn't keep the mad out of my voice.

"Yes," he said, "I would've. And I wouldn't look for you to apologize or explain for a decision you'd made."

Maybe not, I thought, but he had no way of knowing. It was one thing to make a decision that risked his life; it was another to risk mine and Bradford's and Grafton's. And all to fetch a woman who just happened to make her living by opening her legs to anyone who could pay.

If I'd thought things would have changed if I'd said this, I would have, but now the deed was done. We'd all survived, and Halifax had to live with his choice. He might be able to hide who his woman was from himself and strangers, but I knew he'd never be able to hide it from his mama. And that was his problem.

"Listen, Josh," he said. "I need you to understand I wouldn't have shot no one unless I had to. I'm no killer. That cowboy in Dora's drew on me first. I admit I was upset, and putting a couple of extra bullets in him didn't make him any deader, but the fight was fair. And the sheriff, you could see for yourself, that was self-defense."

At first I only paid attention to his idea of self-defense. It didn't seem to me that you could plead self-defense for shooting somebody when you were in the middle of breaking out of jail. Then I felt a hole grow in my belly. "The sheriff?"

Halifax didn't seem to grasp the gravity of what he'd done. "I didn't know who he was at first. I had Rachel by the hand; we were coming out of her room. I guess we were making a lot of noise, or at least enough to wake the folks next door, 'cause just as we get into the hall, the door next to us opens, and this man looks out, naked as a jaybird. I got no idea who he is, I just wave my gun at him, and he ducks back inside, and me and Rachel start going down the stairs. I hear something behind me and I look back, and the naked man had pants and a shirt on, and he had a gun out and was coming after us. That's when I saw his badge. I tried to run for it, but I couldn't move as fast as I wanted with Rachel. Still, I wouldn't have fired if he hadn't. But he did, and I fired back. I had no choice."

I was trying to keep from falling into the hole in my belly. "You think he's dead?"

Halifax shrugged. "I hope not. But usually when men fall like he did, it means they're dead."

He looked at me, his face open and innocent.

"You shot the sheriff," I managed.

"He wasn't much of a lawman," Halifax said. "And, Lord knows, I didn't want to."

I went to tell Bradford. Storm clouds grew in his face. "All of it for a whore," he said. "This all started because of a son-of-a-bitching whore. Now we're knee-deep in muddy water, with a price on our heads."

"What do we do?"

"Watch our back. Chances of them coming after us for killing a lawman are a lot better than if it was just some cowboy. We're liable to have a heap more trouble before this is over."

"My Lord," I said.

"Come on," Bradford said. "We got to move this herd."

Driving those cattle occupied my mind most of the time, but I kept wandering into spaces where everything that had happened in the past few days spun and demanded attention. I'd look at the sky and the land, at the plodding herd, the men who stubbornly moved them. All this had begun as a dream that was tidy and straightforward, but I kept running into violence. Now, me and my brothers were fugitives from the law, something I'd have never thought possible when we left Missouri. We'd broken a man out of jail. That man had killed a sheriff. Still, the idea that a posse was after us was unthinkable, a bad mistake in a land where small mistakes could be fatal. We were black men in a white man's world, and we'd left a white sheriff dead in a doorway in Laredo.

I turned and looked behind me. There was no posse out there, at least none I could see, but the facts were real. How could I keep all of this from Amelia? And what would be the sense of claiming my dream of Montana if she weren't part of it?

I kept the questions at bay for the rest of the day. In the evening, I stayed with the men and listened to their lies and laughter well into the night. I slept and dreamed of Amelia. I had to get to her across a wide, dark space, and her head was turned when I reached her. I pulled her into my arms, and the feel of her flesh was the feel of Halifax's whore.

I ignored the dream. All the next day my head felt thick, my body was tired, and I worked without thinking. I got through the day, and the next one, and the one after that, focusing on the tasks at hand, and the herd moved steady, and nothing came up behind us. We were averaging ten miles a day, and Bradford said we were two and a half days out of Indian country. If we could get there we'd be safe, because no posse would follow.

I appreciated that our luck seemed to have changed, but that evening after supper, Bradford rode back into camp with the news. As he did every day, he'd double back on our trail, find high ground and check to see if we were followed. For the past several days there'd been no sign, but now there was one. The cloud of dust was large. Bradford guessed there were twenty or thirty men hot on the trail behind us.

"What'll we do?" I asked.

"Get to the Indians before that posse gets to us."

I looked at the line of cattle stretching more than a mile, at the wagon, and the horses. "How we going to do that?"

Bradford looked at me like I was the cause of all the

trouble. "I got to think about it. But in the meantime, let's move this herd a little faster."

He walked away, and I heard him say, "All for a son-of-a-bitching whore."

Then he spun, and glared back at where I was standing, frozen by worry and my extreme dislike for him.

"Let's go," he barked. "Move out."

So we moved that herd faster across the brown and dusty land. I couldn't help but think that at this pace the cattle wouldn't be anything more than skin and bone by the time we got to Abilene, that I was leaving me and my brother's profits to melt by the side of the trail. Of course, if we didn't deal with what was behind us, we'd gain no profit at all, only a long time in a Texas prison, or the noose of a hanging rope.

That night we set camp at the base of a bluff in the shadow of Texas trees, and rich range grass and an ample stream of water. The cattle ate and drank, and then folded their legs beneath them. I sat in front of a fire with Seth and the lovely whore. I watched the dance of flames and tried not to look at her. She and Seth were talking low and when she laughed at something he'd said she threw her head back and the length of her neck was exposed. It felt like an offering, and when I looked again, her eyes dropped from mine, and she turned her head away.

I could hear the cowboys on night watch singing to the herd. One voice, clear and high as a woman's, crossed the distance like a bell. I was thinking how strange it was that a beast as dumb as a cow could be soothed by singing.

In the western sky a wide, red band had been left by the falling sun. Above the red the heavens arched in a purple sheet that turned deep black above us. A beautiful woman sat across from me, there were fire and song, and a sky that would make a king humble. Two thousand head of cattle were waiting to make my fortune, and I should have known some peace.

But we'd chosen to break Halifax out of jail, and he was black and had killed a white lawman. I didn't know which was the greater crime, but my instincts said his color. We lived in a country that had gone to war over that.

And now men were coming to take us back to Laredo, for a trial, if we were lucky, and to lynch us if we weren't.

So I had no peace.

Bradford came out of the shadows behind the chuckwagon and said, "I need to talk to you."

I followed him away from the fire's comfort, toward a tangle of fallen trees cut down by Texas weather. He sat on one of the logs, staring into the night. When I turned toward his looking, the campfire glowed like a star.

He broke a piece from the dead tree about the thickness of two fingers and the length of his foot. He stripped the bark from the wood, and I thought of peeling skin, and the wood was white in the dimness. Then he took out his pocketknife and started whittling. As the pale shavings floated down into darkness, he spit and began to hum.

The tune was from my childhood, one of those driving songs sung by slaves in the South of my memory. Field hollers, they were called, except my foreman was singing his real low. I could hear the soft stomp of his foot keeping a steady time.

I was waiting for Bradford to talk, but I was damned if I was going to let him know his not talking was annoying. I sat on the other end of the log, stretched my legs in front of me and couldn't see my feet. I was prepared to be silent as long as my foreman chose to keep humming.

"I think I got a plan," he said.

I waited.

"We take two of our men. Give 'em two days' supply of food and water, the best horses we got. Couple of Winchesters and plenty of ammunition."

He paused. At first I thought he'd lost the thread of his thinking, but he was waiting for me to respond.

I grunted. It wasn't much of a response, but I guess it was all he needed.

"We send them back at the posse. The posse'll camp in a place that provides protection, up against the side of a hill or a bluff, or a place like this one. Our men will open fire at dawn, keep 'em pinned down. Then they'll take off in a direction away from us, heading southeast. There's a spot about two days' ride from here, a canyon with false trails. You could spend three or four days turning in circles if you don't know where you're going. I'll tell the men how to get out, and they'll double back to us. That'll buy us a little time. In the meantime, you and I ride ahead, make contact with the Indians. We'll negotiate passage through their land. Part of the price we'll pay is for them to stop the men behind us."

"Stop them?"

He said, "A show of force is all that ought to be necessary. Those aren't lawmen behind us. Or hired guns. They're farmers and clerks and store owners, with wives and kids to get back to. The minute they see the odds are against them, they'll go back the way they came."

I considered what he'd said. "You think it'll work?"

"Not necessarily," he said, "but I can't come up with nothing else. You got some ideas?"

I said I didn't. "Who you going to send?"

"Luke. And one of the Mexicans. Petey, I think. Both are good horsemen."

I tried not to think of the obvious. The men might be

killed, leaving us a couple of hands short. The posse might not fall for the trick. Even if they did, the Indians might not agree to Bradford's proposal. I told myself I had no control over any of it. If the worst happened, it happened. The worst was an option life kept for itself, like the hidden card in the palm of a crooked gambler.

I didn't want to admit how relieved I was that Bradford hadn't suggested that I go, or one of my brothers. I pulled my feet closer to my body so I could see them. Somehow this made me feel better.

Bradford tossed the whittled wood into the darkness, folded his knife, and went to tell the men of their mission. I strolled back to the fire, which had burned down to red-hot embers. The beautiful whore had gone off someplace, probably to be with Halifax. Seth was inside the wagon, getting things together for the morning. I called good night to him, took my bedroll and spread it on the ground where the rest of the men were sleeping. I lay on my back for a while, staring at the sky. I whispered a good night to Amelia. I rolled onto my side and slept, and when I woke up, it was raining.

CHAPTER TEN

It was a driving rain that came out of the northwest at a slant that stung our faces.

"We head out in this?" I asked Bradford.

"It'll work to our advantage. Slow the posse down. They won't move till it blows over."

He turned away from a wind that wouldn't stop to catch its breath. "It won't last through the afternoon," he said. "We'll get this herd across the Brazos. Then you and I go ahead and talk to the Indians."

"We're crossing a river in this?"

"You're already wet," he said.

I looked at him. For a moment I thought he was smiling, but he was squinting from the rain in his eyes.

We got the cattle to the Brazos a little after noon. The water was brown and swirling. The rain had slowed to a drizzle, and the wind that hadn't paused for breathing had died a quiet death.

When we reached the river, we had an awkward moment. Cowboys get naked to drive a herd across a river. And we had a woman in our midst. I thought it was funny that the men would be modest with a whore. None of them had anything she hadn't seen a hundred times before.

Bradford solved the problem by sending Seth and Rachel across the river first. He told Seth to go for a mile or so and set up for the midday meal.

Shouts from the cowboys crowded the day as we moved the herd into the water. Several head took off downstream, and we had a few bad minutes until we got them back.

On the other side of the river, we stopped for our midday meal. We ate with the stench of two thousand drenched longhorns in our throats. Around three o'clock the rain stopped, just like Bradford had said. The sky cleared, and the sun came out. We pushed the herd for another five miles. When evening fell, we made camp in an open space. The cattle were quiet, and the sky was clear except for the stars that lived there.

The next morning, just before sunup, Bradford and I headed out to meet the Indians. We rode all day, stopping only to water the horses. The sun hammered my head and beat on my neck and shoulders.

In the evening we ate dried beef and biscuits. We unrolled our blankets and slept near the edge of a stream. I slept hard, without dreaming, and it was dark when Bradford shook me. We ate cold biscuits and drank stream water and covered ten miles before dawn. We were going hard and fast, and Bradford wasn't talking. That was all right with me. I needed all the energy I had to stand up to our punishing pace.

At the end of the second day, I'd seen three things that looked like Indians. One turned out to be a cactus that had waved to us from a distance. Another was a couple of jackrabbits spooked by our horses, and the last was a gathering of tumbleweed the size of a newborn calf. The weed went spinning across the Texas plains and had me reaching for my pistol.

When we camped for the night, I asked Bradford how much farther we had to go to reach Indian territory.

"Let's see," he said. He threw his head back like he was figuring. "Two weeks."

"Two weeks? We going to be away from the herd for two weeks? In two weeks that posse'll have come and gone. We can't wait two weeks."

"You asked me how far it was to Indian territory. That's two weeks, near as I can figure."

"Two weeks is too much time," I said.

"We ain't going all the way to Indian territory. We'll ride one more day. Then we'll stop and make a fire."

I thought my foreman had lost his mind. "A fire? What's a fire going to do?"

"You'll see," he said. "Now you better get some sleep. We got another hard day of riding before us."

And that's what we did the next morning, got up before dawn, ate cold biscuits and canteen water, saddled our horses, and continued our journey north. I don't remember too much of that day, except it was hot and dry, and the sky stretched in this uncaring, stainless blue. Once a solitary hawk spiraled high above us, as if it was lost or sad.

I was well on the other side of being tired, and my body seemed connected by flesh to my horse. I wondered again how things had gotten so fouled up, and if I was right to trust Bradford.

We stopped at midday to rest our horses, and my foreman slept while I watched. Then we were up again, heading toward a line of ridges in the distance, and we reached them just before dusk. We ate a meal I'd grown to hate—cold biscuits, water, and dried beef—and I was tired enough to fall asleep without trouble.

It seemed I'd just closed my eyes when Bradford put a rough hand on my shoulder. I got up into the cool of almost morning, moving from habit, rolling my blanket, staggering to saddle my horse.

"That won't be necessary just yet," Bradford said.

I rubbed sleep from my eyes. "What won't be necessary?"

"Your horse."

"Why?"

"We ain't riding. We're collecting wood."

"*Wood?*"

"Firewood."

For a moment the world tilted at a silly angle, and then I remembered Bradford had said something the day before about a fire. I looked around me, and day began to break with light as rare as a miracle. I didn't pay it any mind. I was thinking of firewood and how at least we wouldn't have to travel to fetch it. We'd camped in a grove where limbs were scattered across the ground, and plenty of brush and twigs for kindling. In some places it looked like men, not nature, had carefully piled the fuel.

"We got to move it up there."

I looked to where Bradford pointed, at the top of the tallest ridge before us, some thirty feet in the air. From where I stood, it looked like a wall. "How we going to get up there?"

"Walk," Bradford said. "Lessen you can fly."

I considered telling him where he could go to deposit the back portion of his body. I considered informing him about the illegitimate origins of certain of his family members. I imagined busting him in his face.

I bent to the gathering of wood. When I had an armful, I turned and found Bradford staring at me like I wore two hats, or was buck naked in the morning.

"Take your blanket," he said. "Tie up the wood in that. That way you have one arm for holding when you climb."

I dumped my armful on the ground, kicked at it. "You could've told me that before," I said. "Instead of standing there like some thank you, Mr. Bossman–slave master. It'd be nice to feel like we're in this together, Bradford. Why you acting like the enemy?"

"I ain't no enemy." He sounded disappointed. "I'd a thought you had sense enough to know that by now."

"What's your problem?"

He sighed. "I got no problem. I got responsibility." He took the first finger of his right hand and began to poke it into the cup of his left. "I got two thousand head of cattle and a crew I got to get in one piece to Abilene. I got a price on my head 'cause a boy what thinks with his dick killed two men, and one of them was a sheriff. I got a posse out there coming to take me back to a white man's justice. I'm standing here in the middle of Texas with a man who needs his hand held. But I got no problem."

"Ain't nobody keeping you against your will," I said. "You can leave any time you want."

He looked at me. He looked at me some more, and shook his head.

"Sure I can. And then where the hell would you be?"

He snorted in disgust. He bent to wood, and I to mine, although my head was hot with other than sunlight, and my visions of strangling him made me tremble.

When we had a load we knotted our blankets, and began to climb that ridge. It was bad, but not nearly as bad as I'd thought. A couple of times my foot slipped, and I feared I was a goner, but I managed to find a handhold and a solid place for my feet.

The view from the top was the sameness of Texas country, as if God had run out of ideas. We made two more trips up and down that ridge and then we piled the wood and lit it. When it was burning good, Bradford took his blanket and began waving at the flames. Huge clouds of smoke sailed into the featureless sky, like the heads of rotten mushrooms.

I asked, "How do you know they're out there?"

"Who?"

"The Indians."

"They're out there."

"What you saying to them?"

"Help."

He was beating that fire like to beat the band, and smoke bubbles the size of calves sailed across Texas like they knew where they were going.

When he put his blanket down, we sat until the fire had burned to ashes. Then Bradford picked up his blanket, folded it like he had just washed it in a river. I was glad he hadn't used mine. His was going to stink from smoke until a week before Kingdom come.

"What we do now?"

"Go back to the horses. And wait."

"What if they don't come?"

"They'll come."

For the rest of the day we stayed put, and time moved only when it had to. I told myself that the rest was good for me and good for the horses, but the truth is I hate to wait.

I tried to fill the time. I dozed. I brushed my horse. I cleaned my gun and my rifle. I wrote a letter to Amelia. I ate that damned dried beef and another biscuit and dozed again. I thought about the saying "time stood still," and I kicked at it to get it moving.

I took the first watch that night while Bradford slept. When he relieved me, I thought I'd have trouble sleeping, but I went off like a baby. I think it was because sleeping was something to do, and time speeds up while you do it.

When Bradford woke me, it was light. I sat up, rubbing my eyes, and then I felt my stomach open. Fear seared a path from my throat to where my legs met in the middle.

A group of Indians stood watching me, thirty or forty of them at least, big men and strong and silent. They were armed with knives and six-guns, Winchesters.

I made a move for my gun, and Bradford grabbed my arm. "It's all right. This the safest you been since you got to Texas."

I tried to control my breathing.

"What we do now?" I said, and when my face moved, I felt my scalp tingle.

"Saddle up. Head back to the herd."

And that's what we did, me and Bradford riding by ourselves in a pace much more leisurely than the one that had marked our coming, the Indians to our left, maybe fifty yards away.

Bradford explained what had happened while I slept. The Indians had shown up just before light, a combination hunting and scouting party whose responsibility, in addition to providing meat for their village, was to monitor the approach to their territory, to know when cattle drives were coming, and to negotiate for passage through their land. As Bradford had known they would, they'd seen his signals. They'd agreed to the price he'd offered, and agreed, as a personal favor to him, to frighten off the posse. Well, not totally as a personal favor: he'd had to double the price.

"How much?"

"Ten head to go through their territory. Ten head to take care of the posse. And I threw in another five for good measure."

"What do they do with cattle?"

"Eat 'em."

I was quiet for a while, wondering how much profit this would cost me. Then I looked to my right, where Bradford rode beside me, his face as expressionless as a rock.

"How'd you talk to them?" I said.

"What?" He looked at me like I had interrupted something he'd been finding pleasure in thinking.

"The Indians. How'd you talk to them?"

"What do you mean how'd I talk to them?" He was looking at me again like I was naked.

"I mean do you know their language?"

"How do you think I talked to them if I didn't?"

"Well, where'd you learn to speak it?"

"I lived with them for a while." He shook his head. He spurred his horse and rode ahead of me, his shoulders up around his ears.

I sighed. As annoying as my foreman could be, he could always find a way to surprise me. The first time had been when he spoke Spanish to Romero. I wondered how long ago he'd lived with Indians, and why, and if he'd ever tell me. I wondered what else about Bradford was waiting to make me wonder. Maybe he'd been to Europe and had dined with the King of England. Maybe he'd been to Paris and spoke French.

That thought brought a smile to my face. I let my horse drift a little to the left so that I divided in half the space between me and the Indians. I'd seen Indians in St. Louis, and I'd seen them from afar on my way to Texas. But I'd never seen so many at one time, up close in their own land, acting like they were in charge. It struck me as both odd and inaccurate that they were called "red." These had a range of colors not much different than Negroes had. Several were my complexion, some darker. The features that most distinguished them were the sharpness of their faces, and their hair, which was straight and black. I'd have to ask Bradford what kind of Indians they were.

I looked around at the Texas countryside. I looked above me at the blue, blue sky that was clear except for some wispy clouds in the far-off southeast corner. I saw a hawk floating like a lazy swimmer. Way off to the west buzzards circled as if waiting for something to die.

I felt better. I was on my way back to the herd, and my brothers, and the reasonable expectation that we'd make it to Abilene with no trouble once we'd scared the posse off. Nobody had died in my presence in the last couple of days. I didn't think about the fact that I was a wanted man, and my brother had killed a sheriff, and that whether or not we faced man's justice, we still had to answer to God. I guess I was hoping that God would understand and give us a break. I hoped He'd seen that we hadn't intended to get into trouble. We just wanted to drive a herd of cattle to Abilene, sell them, and then I would take my woman to Montana where the sky stretched forever and live the life I'd dreamed of. We'd raise a family and love each other, and when I died, years and years and years from now, I'd leave it all to my kids.

For the time being, and as far into the future as I could imagine, I was young and healthy, full to the brim with choices. Right now I was riding with Indians, and I'd have a story to tell when I got back to Missouri. I didn't think at all of consequences. I only thought of the dream.

*   *   *

When we camped that evening, Bradford said we were less than a half day's ride from the herd. The Indians kept to themselves, built their own fire, sat around it like ordinary folks, laughing and talking in language I didn't understand.

When I'd eaten my biscuit and beef, and washed it down with canteen water, I picked up a stick to add up what Indian help was costing. Bradford watched me. He was biting on a small twig he'd been using to clean his teeth. I could tell he wanted to know what I was doing, but he wouldn't give me the satisfaction of asking. He liked being the one with the answers.

I bent to my figuring. When I was done, I whistled my surprise.

"What you whistling at?" Bradford said. His curiosity had got to him.

"The cost of having Indian help."

"How much is it?"

"Nine hundred twenty dollars."

"How'd you figure it?"

"Simple. Figure out what it cost to buy the cattle. Subtract that from what they'll bring in Abilene."

"You figure out the cost if that posse catch up to us?"

I started to tell him that I wasn't questioning his decision, I was just a businessman adding up the cost of what I bought. But before I could say that, Bradford made a disgusted noise in his throat.

"You figure the cost if the Indians decided no more cattle through their territory?"

I hated the tone he was using, that godawful know-it-all tone that ticked me off.

"Yeah," I said. "About thirty cents."

He looked at me like I was crazy.

"That was a joke, Bradford."

"Then how come it ain't funny?"

"Maybe you got no sense of humor."

"I got a sense of humor. I just know the difference be-tween funny and stupid."

"Now I'm stupid."

"No," he said. "You ain't stupid now. You *been* stupid. Can't figure out how a man who can read and write can be so dumb. Give reading and writing a bad name."

"I can't figure it out either, Bradford, but as soon as we finish driving these cattle, I'll set my mind to it. Let me know where you are, so I can write you and tell you the answer. You can have somebody read it to you."

He was stung. "You can kiss a Indian's red ass," he said.

"They ain't red," I said. "Different shades of brown."

"You can kiss it anyway." And he got up and walked away.

I sat and watched the night fall. Part of me felt that I'd made a mistake in insulting Bradford, part of me didn't give a damn.

I never heard him return. If he did, it was while I was sleeping.

CHAPTER ELEVEN

In the morning, I tried to make it up to Bradford. I didn't like myself for having insulted him. I could have been angry at him in a different way. I also knew that being on the outs with my trail boss wasn't the best way to guarantee getting a herd to Abilene. Sure, he was a pain in the butt, but he was a good man. He hadn't made one decision that I could quarrel with besides insisting that we shoot those rustlers, and the truth was, I understood the sense in what he'd said. It was me who had the problem with killing.

So I went over to him to beg his pardon.

"Much obliged," he said, "but you ain't hurt my feelings. I'll let you know if you hurt my feelings."

We saddled up at dawn, rode hard, and just before we would have stopped for the midday meal, Avery, who was riding point for the day, cantered out of the south. I think he had a bad moment when he saw the Indians, but he controlled himself, and came to meet us.

"How's the herd?" Bradford asked.

"Fine. Moving at a good clip, seven miles back. I see you brought some help."

Bradford nodded. "How'd the plan work? Petey and Luke back?"

Avery shook his head. "Luke got back all right, but they got Petey."

"Shit," Bradford said. "They got Petey? Luke able to bring him back?"

Avery shook his head.

"Bury him?"

"Nope."

Bradford seemed to sag a little.

Avery said, "Posse's no more than a half a day behind us. Figure they'll hit us at dawn."

"We'll be ready," Bradford said. He rode off to talk to the Indians, and after a few minutes, they headed east at a gallop.

Bradford rode back to us.

"Why they heading east?" I asked.

"Circling the herd. Then they'll ride west and south and find a place to stand off the posse."

We turned toward camp and got there just as Seth had started to clean up after the midday meal. He grumbled, but he fed us.

The men were tense that evening. One of their own had died. They'd hadn't counted on this kind of trouble, being part of a drive where half their sidekicks were wanted for murder and breaking a man out of jail. They hadn't planned on being pursued by a posse with four times as many men as we had. Besides, even if the odds had been better, they weren't gunmen; they were cowboys. Most of them didn't want any more excitement than the world spinning when they'd drained another whiskey bottle.

They were particularly bothered that a whore was at the bottom of it all. Whores, they'd said, were a dime a dozen, to be used and discarded, to be replaced by one who was younger and prettier, even if she cost a little more.

Before now, they'd been polite to Rachel. I thought that it had to do with Bradford's warning that he'd have the head of any man who interfered with her, or their knowing that Halifax had already shot two men because of her. But their reaction seemed to have to do only with Rachel. They'd treated her with a respect that would have been at home in churches, tipped their hats in her presence, watched their language, and generally acted as much like gentlemen as they could. But now they went out of their way to avoid her.

I needed these men, needed their commitment and loyalty and skills, and so, after I talked to Bradford about it, I told them all that had happened was unfortunate and not their fault. I said I hadn't meant to see a situation created that put their lives in danger. I reminded them that Halifax had shot both men in self-defense, and that because he was a black man, only two possibilities existed for his getting a fair trial: slim and none. That a sheriff had been shot was bad business, but each of them would understand that if a man fired at you, you didn't stop to find out if he was wearing a badge before you fired back. Anyway, we weren't sure the sheriff was dead.

I told the men to rest assured that all of that was behind us. The Indians would send the posse back where they'd come from, and we'd get on to the business at hand, which was to drive these cattle to Abilene.

Still, I said, I knew that the job had become more difficult due to the reasons I'd just stated, and I was going to give each man an additional five-dollar-a-week bonus when the drive was over.

I wasn't crazy about further eating into my profits, but I figured it was a good business decision. I can't say that the

men were overjoyed by my announcement, but some nodded their heads, and some smiled with figuring out how
much pleasure the additional money would buy.

Halifax came over to me after my talk. He said it was
his fault, that he'd brought all the trouble on us, and it
wasn't fair that the extra pay for the cowhands would come
out of our collective profits. He said he'd pay the extra out
of his share.

"Halifax," I said, "I ain't happy with what you did, but
I understand how it happened. We're in this together. We
started out together, and we'll finish together, and we'll
share and share alike."

He looked at me like he was trying to read between my
words. "I'm glad you're my brother," he said.

I nodded. "I'm glad you're mine."

It was a touching scene, but it wasn't honest. I wasn't
happy that Halifax's lethal attraction for a whore had got
us into trouble in the first place. He'd shown bad judgment,
and I knew it would be a long time before I trusted him
again.

But it wasn't the time or place to say this. I didn't need
my brother walking around with the weight of the world
on his shoulders, and I didn't need him ticked off at me. I
had a hard enough time dealing with Bradford. It was my
responsibility to hold this undertaking together.

Night came, and I realized how worn out I was, and
when I lay down, I slept hard for what seemed like a minute. Then Bradford was shaking me, saying it was time to
go.

It was so dark I could barely make out his face.

"Where we going?" I whispered.

"With the Indians to meet the posse."

"What for?"

"Make sure everything goes right."

I rolled out of my blanket, pulled my boots on, and we went to saddle two horses. I was wondering why he hadn't told me the night before.

"You don't trust the Indians?" I said.

"They got services to sell. Just making sure we're the highest bidder."

I swung onto my horse, looked out over the herd that filled the dark like a wide and restless ghost, and we rode to meet the Indians. No greetings were exchanged. We just headed south for an hour while dawn painted gray streaks in the arc of a deep blue sky, and we came to the ambush spot.

I had to admit it was perfect. The trail wound through two walls of hills that left a space wide enough for maybe four men across on horseback. The walls were so sheer I doubted that goats could climb them.

The Indians scattered, took up positions that made a semicircle. From where me and Bradford were, you couldn't see them. They were out there, more than thirty strong, but they were as invisible and as silent as a thought.

Then I was doing it again, stretched out on the ground, waiting. Maybe that's just the way life was out here, you spent a lot of it waiting. Or maybe waiting was a big part of life in general, and I'd had to break the hold of a small, safe farm outside of Springfield to learn this.

I turned toward the east where the sky was whispering with dawn's weak pinkish light. Bradford nudged me. "Here they come," he said.

I strained to see where he'd pointed. I could hear the muffled sounds of hoofbeats, but the light hadn't reached the canyon walls. It was like looking into a tunnel, and I blinked, and then I could see them coming. They rode easily, not identifiable as men on horseback, just a mass of moving shadows. As they entered the mouth of the canyon, the sun began to rise.

I figured the length of the passage was about a quarter of a mile. When the last of the posse had cleared the entrance, I heard the crack of a rifle. There was enough light now for me to see the bullet kick up dust a yard in front of the lead rider. His horse reared and turned, and he fought to control it. Behind him, men on horseback were milling, their faces, the features of which I still couldn't see, turned to the top of the canyon. Another shot rang out, and some of the posse drew their weapons, and I heard a shout and the men were dismounting, looking for protection.

There was little protection. A boulder that could safeguard two bodies, a shallow gully that could hide several more. Farther up the sides of the slopes huddled trees and brush and ledges that afforded shelter, but I knew that unless the men panicked, they wouldn't move toward them. They'd be picked off before they got there.

I heard a whistle like a bird call carving up the morning, and when it was answered, the top of the canyon came alive with a picket fence of Indians holding their rifles pointed down below. The posse saw them, and they looked to the north, to their right, their left, and they looked behind them. Everywhere they turned, Indians stood silhouetted against the sky.

The lead rider held his hand up in a motion that said, "Be still." The hand was huge and impossibly white. I could feel my heart pounding, and my palms began to sweat. One of the Indians approached the posse, riding at a slow and stately walk. Halfway there, he stopped and turned his pony in a circle, then moved forward again. He stopped, repeated the movement.

"What's he doing?" I whispered to Bradford.

"Showing he's not holding a weapon."

I don't know why I looked at the sky. It was a blue so fresh it looked brand-new, and the sun was like a blessing.

I turned back to what was below me. The Indian had stopped, gesturing in a manner that suggested he was speaking. One of the posse came forward. I'd expected it to be the man with the large white hand, but it wasn't. I scanned the posse, but I couldn't make him out.

"Now he's telling them they're surrounded," Bradford said. "He'll let that sink in for a moment, let them feel the fear of it. Then he'll tell them they're free to go, so long as it's back to where they come from. He'll tell them not to move until he's gotten back up here, so that none of his friends will get nervous and mistake the movement for attack."

The Indian had turned to ride back the way he'd come, still moving in that slow and stately walk. When he got to the point in the trail where a huge boulder threw an egg-shaped shadow, he raised his right arm and brought it sharply down.

"Shit," Bradford said.

I didn't have time to ask him why he cursed. In the next second I had no need to ask, because the day was shattered by the rapid fire of rifles.

I wasn't close enough to see faces, but I was close enough to see blood spurt when bullets struck horse or man. I was close enough to see human heads explode, and the cries of dying men rode the air like the most desperate of curses. The horses reared and screamed and fell, and the men used them for barricades, firing back with the same results they'd have gotten from shooting at the sky.

I didn't understand why the Indians had attacked. I could tell from Bradford's face that *he* didn't either. "Like shooting fish in a barrel," he said. His voice made me think of a sinner who'd just been converted.

"Get back to the herd," he barked. "Leave Seth and four men to watch, bring the rest."

"For what?"

"We got to bury 'em."

I looked at him. He was shaking with rage. Whether it was directed at me, or the Indians, or the posse, or the thought of having to bury dead men, I didn't know. I swung onto my horse. I dug my heels into its flanks, and galloped toward the herd.

I rode about thirty minutes, and when I looked to my right, I saw the Indians moving north, taking with them the horses that had survived the massacre. They didn't seem to be in any hurry. I rode another fifteen minutes, and then I looked behind me. Buzzards, black in the sky, were circling the corpses.

I kicked my horse hard. When I reached camp, I filled Seth in.

"They wiped out the posse?"

"To a man," I answered.

"They was only supposed to scare them."

"That's what I thought."

"You reckon Bradford really knows how to speak Injun? Maybe he mixed up what he was saying."

I shrugged.

"This ain't good," Seth said. "You know somebody's going to want an accounting for what happened to that posse."

"Seth, I got the same questions you have. Pull some shovels out of that wagon, will you? I'll go get the men."

I rode out to the herd and got six of the hands. When I told them what had happened, their faces grew worried. Here was more trouble they hadn't counted on.

"You can't trust Injuns," one said. "Anybody knows

that. We're going to have every lawman in Texas looking for us.''

I didn't answer. I hoped he wasn't right. I sent a man out to the point so the lead rider would know what was happening.

When I got back to Seth, the Indians were coming toward us. When they reached a small grove, they stopped, dismounted. Some of them stretched out on the ground. Some sat. Some stood looking back toward the place they'd come from.

"What you reckon they're waiting for?" Seth said.

"To get paid."

"If I had my way," Seth sputtered, "they wouldn't get one red cent. Not a head."

I said, "We'll let Bradford handle that."

I headed with the men back to Bradford. All the way there my eyes were held by the soaring, circling buzzards. By the time we reached the canyon, the birds were more bold, came closer. Bradford was firing at them with his rifle. They'd fly away a little, then return.

He stood up when we reached him.

"Well, I know why," he said.

"Why what?" I said.

"Why the Indians opened fire."

I waited. The men were staring down at the carnage, dead men and horses, bloodied and smashed. One of them softly cursed.

Bradford said, "That wasn't no posse. That was Steele."

"Steele?" The little man who'd called me a nigger, whose hands I'd smashed.

"Yup. Kept his promise to come after you. Must've been a pretty deep mad to bring him this close to Indian territory. But I reckon he figured he'd catch up to us before he met up with them." He paused. "Well, whatever he figured, he was wrong. *Dead* wrong." He swallowed and shook his head. "They didn't scalp anyone but him.

"Come on," he said, "let's go bury 'em before every buzzard in Texas comes calling."

We moved down the hill, approached the dead and grisly bodies, horseflesh and human, what was once alive, and strong, and dreaming. I wandered among the dead until I found Steele. Those were the hands I'd smashed, wrapped in bandages that had made them seem so large and white to me from a distance. He was on his back, arms spread as if in crucifixion, the top of his head sliced away. I'd never seen a scalped man. Flies buzzed along his forehead. Blood streamed down his face in crusted lines. Some of it had collected in the hollow of his throat. His eyes were open. I thought about saying a prayer for the dead, but the words wouldn't come when I tried.

It was then it hit me. Instead of dread, I felt a steady calm. I'd watched the slaughter without the hole forming in my stomach. I'd felt no sickness, and no red wall had come up behind my eyes. I remembered that when Halifax had shot the sheriff, I'd had no reaction to that, either. Something had happened in me, and I wondered what it was. I had a deep feeling it was bad, and now my knees shook.

I took a deep breath and joined the cowboys and dragged bodies to the gully. We worked long and hard and nobody spoke, and the buzzards silently watched us. We covered the men with dirt and rock. They were bad men, rustlers and thieves and probably a murderer or two. Their leader had killed women and children. Still, it was a terrible way to die.

I started to protest when some of the men rifled the dead men's pockets, took boots, collected guns. They looked at me, and I held my tongue.

We dragged the men to the gully, we threw them in, we covered them with dirt and rocks. We left the dead horses for the buzzards who were shivering with anticipation, their obscene faces alive with what I took for joy.

I wondered if I'd done the right thing in coming to Texas. But I couldn't spend much time thinking. I had to bury the dead. It was a hard job, and all the while I did it, I felt the need for prayer.

CHAPTER TWELVE

For days what had happened in the canyon hung above us like a curse. The men were subdued. I think the task of burying strangers far from friends and loved ones reminded them of what could be their fate. I know some were ashamed of rifling the bodies. I saw boots and belts and a handgun or two left beneath brush or rock, as if to keep them would be to keep evidence of sin.

The weather unfolded in hot, calm days, blue skies with fluffy clouds. The nights were cool, star-studded, good for sleeping. We took advantage of the weather and averaged ten miles a day, and the sun was ever changing high above us, sometimes a rare gold coin, sometimes a globe that in the evening wore deep purple, red, and yellow. When the sun set, the moon arrived, a crescent with points as sharp as steer horns. Days passed, and the moon seemed a living thing that ate stars and night and swelled toward its fullness.

By the end of the week the men were looser, as if the sun had baked away bad memories, and they were lulled by the steady progress, the feeding moon. Except for Bradford. He was all business, admonishing us to keep our eye on the task before us.

I'd tried to stay away from Bradford, and he'd made it easy by avoiding me. I thought he was still stung from my calling attention to the fact he couldn't read. Well, I'd apologized for that, and if he refused to accept my apology, I couldn't do anything about it. Staying out of his way meant that I didn't have to subject myself to his irritating habits.

After four days, I changed my mind about avoiding him. The drive was still my undertaking, and if Bradford's seriousness was related to concerns I wasn't aware of, it was my responsibility to know.

I'll give him credit. When I approached him, he managed to talk to me without the weight of resignation slumping his shoulders, without the disbelief on his face that suggested I was slightly dumber than a longhorn. He said this was dangerous country and driving cattle serious work. The fact that the weather had eased, and we were making good time, and no misfortune had recently befallen us was no excuse for relaxing. Anything could happen.

When I asked him what anything was, he said just that, *anything*, a stampede, a sudden change in the weather. The cattle could come down with fever, the men could get sick, or we could be set upon by rustlers. We'd left two dead men back in Laredo, and it was reasonable to expect that someone someday would come after us. We'd be more than lucky if no one did.

Finally, we'd left a mess of dead men back in a canyon, and although he wasn't suspicious, he'd lived long enough to know that kind of thing often brought bad luck. That's why he was careful, why he rode off each evening to find high ground so he could look to see if we were followed. So far no one had appeared, but that didn't mean they wouldn't.

I asked him if there was anything extra I could do, some way I could help.

"Just keep your mind on what we got to do," he said. "Just pay attention."

So I did what he said. I paid attention.

Still, as the days passed, and the men laughed and sang in the evening, and walked with a briskness that spoke of their heightened spirits, I allowed his warning to ease to the back of my mind. I began to feel sure of myself, that what I'd set out to do was right and proper, that the deaths I'd witnessed and been forced to be part of were no fault of mine. I believed we'd make it to Abilene and sell the cattle. I'd move on to the next stage of my life, head for Montana, and make my dream come true.

The steadiness of the drive, the weather, and the good feeling gave me opportunity to consider my brothers. Grafton seemed wrapped in a newfound sense of self and purpose. Maybe he'd always had it, and I hadn't known to look. Maybe my seeing was caused by Bradford's saying that Grafton had good sense and could be counted on. Whatever the reason, it was clear that I no longer needed to think of Grafton as my little brother. He was still fond of teasing and always ready with a laugh, but he was a full-grown man more than able to care for himself.

And Halifax, head over heels in love with a whore whose beauty, I'd decided, was matchless, was calm and easy, and the smile had come back to his face. I still didn't take to the idea of his bringing this woman home to my mama, but I understood there was nothing I could do, so I kept my feelings to myself.

I watched Rachel as she moved among the men. She wore old pants, a shirt she'd gotten from Seth. Her face was scrubbed, and her hair fell in a tail just below her shoulders. The men had gone back to treating her with a formal affection. She did her share of the work, and she adored Halifax. You could tell by the way she looked at him. A couple of times I turned to find her watching me, but she never dropped her eyes, or pretended that she wasn't. She'd just smile, open and friendly.

At other times she had an expression on her face like she was about to say something. When I saw that expression the third time, I asked, "Is everything all right?"

It was an invitation, a door to walk through if she chose. But she said that all was fine.

As the days went by, something lifted from me. It took a while to realize it was nothing more than the sense of responsibility that I had for my brothers. Before we left Missouri, I used to talk to them about the rest of their lives, about the need to prepare for the future. Like most young men, they thought the future was the following morning to be dealt with when they awoke. They'd listen to my speeches with a mixture of respect and good humor and impatience.

But the drive and all that had happened had changed them both. Even though I still believed Halifax had shown bad judgment, I couldn't stay mad at him. He'd made a mistake, but everybody made those, and what was important was that you didn't make it again. And Grafton was as solid as a rock. The sense that I had to watch out for them was replaced by the feeling that we could watch out for each other. And I realized that though I often felt alone, I didn't need to feel that anymore. I had my brothers. We'd become equal partners.

The discovery made me feel strong and in control, sure of myself, which is why, two weeks later, as a few of us sat around the fire after supper, I let my brothers stroke my pride. The conversation had been wide-ranging, stories of the recently fought war, the best way to treat a calf for fever, and then it turned to legendary marksmen: Abner Doubleton out of Baltimore, Rick Sedgeway from Wyoming, my own Caesar, Annie Oakley, and Wyatt Earp. Grafton said that whereas he hadn't seen none of them but Caesar, he'd take his chances on me against the whole lot. After all, Caesar had taught me, and I'd gotten better than Caesar, even Caesar had said so. If anyone wanted to place a wager, Halifax said, he'd bet that nobody could come up with a target I couldn't hit if they could.

All of a sudden, everybody was a marksman, saying they'd been taught by so-and-so. Then the real lying started. Marlon said he'd shot the eye out of a chicken without disturbing the egg it sat on. Simon said once he'd needed a pen to write a letter to his woman. He walked outside and picked out exactly one feather from a soaring hawk. Seth said Simon couldn't write, so what did he need a pen for?

I don't remember who told the tale about a raccoon back home in Illinois that kept eating the greens out of his mama's garden, and how he'd measured the distance so perfect with his shotgun that when he fired the pellet spread was just wide enough to make that raccoon vanish. They never found hide nor hair of the varmint, and his family ate sweet greens through the winter.

"Now what have you done?" they asked me. "What kind of shooting you done that comes even close?"

I thought about the boy in the woods, the drifter I'd shot, but I pushed it from my mind, and though I smiled I didn't answer. I never liked to brag about my shooting. Somehow it seemed that bragging about it was to disrespect that boy. Whatever practicing I did, I did in private. I did think about a couple of lies I could have told, but none was as good as what I'd heard, so I just said, "Well, once I hit the broad side of a barn."

The men got to hooting and hollering that if I was so good I ought to have a story to tell, and Halifax said it was just the way I was, low-key, no-brag, just-do. Them what thought they was so good, he said, should get together the next evening and put up some money, and he and Grafton would back me. We'd see who the real shot was and who the teller of tales.

So the challenge was given, and I took it. The next day, in the lean after-supper light, beneath a pale half-moon that rose across the heaven from a deep red, setting sun, we rode a couple of miles away from the cattle, heeding Bradford's warning to make sure we were far enough so as not to spook the herd. Grafton had gotten a mess of cans from Seth, and we set up targets. We were six, and the bet was two dollars a man with all the money going to the winner. First, a still target that each of us drew our pistols on and fired at. Then, drawing again, firing at a can thrown high in the air. Next, rapid-firing a rifle from fifty paces. The last was shooting from a galloping horse at a can sent rolling across the ground.

By the time the sun had set all the way, and the silver moon was almost straight above us, I'd beat everybody flat out and square and the losers were gracious. I split the money with my brothers, and Halifax slapped me on the back and looked at me with pride in his eyes. We rode back into camp, and all of us were singing, and I was as full as that fat half-moon.

Two more days went by, and the weather stayed fine, the grass and water plentiful, and no one came behind us. The men had bonded all the way, become a tightly knit, efficient team.

I worked hard and slept hard, and before I fell asleep I'd think of Amelia, and sometimes I'd dream of her. Twice I wrote a letter I couldn't send.

Sometimes I'd lie awake at night, just looking at the stars, fussing at myself because I hadn't brought along a book. But most nights I was too tired to read, and besides I'd have had to take guff from the men if they'd seen me reading. To fill the time, I dreamed about Montana. I invented the view from the front porch of the house I'd build, and filled it with the sounds of my children. I'd think of Amelia and, like I said, at times I'd dream of her. The dreams were pleasant, even though sometimes I woke with an edge that called for a woman's touch.

I'd blunt the edge with hard work, and all was right in the world, and Texas was a wonderful place to be, and being alive was special. From time to time, because it's my nature, I had the nagging feeling that it was all too good to be true.

Looking back, I guess it was. I had this talk with Rachel.

We were sitting around a fire, seventeen days out of Abilene, me and Halifax and Rachel, Singer and Burt, not saying much, mostly watching the leaping flames. Once in a while something popped in the fire, and somebody said something, but mostly it was a silence that no one cared to disturb. I watched the shadows of the fire play across Rachel's face where her head leaned against Halifax's shoulder.

Singer stretched and said he was going to turn in, and Burt said he thought he would, too. They left and Halifax remarked what a nice night it was, and I thought he'd already said that, but then I decided that some things were worth repeating, so I allowed as how it was.

Then Halifax said to Rachel, "I'm turning in. You ready?" She hesitated, and then said no, she'd sit here awhile, and Halifax said okay, he'd see her later. He said good night to me, and I thought something was different in his voice, but I couldn't say what exactly.

Maybe this was a setup. Maybe it was tied to the way Rachel sometimes looked at me, as if she wanted to talk. Then I knew as sure as I was sitting there that this was about her going home and having to meet my mama.

While I was figuring out what to do, how to make some kind of civilized conversation, I looked into the darkness, beyond the camp where the cows bedded for the night.

"You don't much like me, do you?"

My first feeling was annoyance. The second was shame. "That's not true," I said, and I realized my heart was pounding.

I made myself look at her. The fire was in her eyes. She was sitting with her legs pulled up against her chest, hands laced beneath knees that made a pillow for her chin. She was dressed the way she always was, in a man's blue shirt and pants, but neither did anything to take away from her beauty. The hat she wore during the day hung down her back, held by the tied ends of leather thongs at her neck, and I was still given to wonder that such a slender column bore the weight of her lovely head. The fire both deepened and brightened the honey in her skin. She had a pair of boots on, solid and sensible, and as I watched, the toe of her left foot moved long enough to make me think she was shivering or drawing in the earth.

"Halifax told me," she said.

"Halifax couldn't have told you nothing I ain't told him," I countered, and I knew she knew I was ducking the point.

"All right," she said. "What *do* you feel about me?"

I swallowed and turned away. "You seem to be a nice person."

She was quiet, and when I looked, her head was tilted, and she wore a faint, beguiling smile.

When she spoke again, her voice was lower, deliberate, as if she spoke from rote, or deep conviction.

"I know what I've done. I ain't proud of it, but I know why I did it. Some people say you're what you do. That may be true if you're doing what you want, but if you ain't, then who you are is what you think." She paused. "That make sense to you?"

"I don't know," I said. "I'll have to study on it."

"Halifax understands that. It's one reason why I love him. He says to blame me for what I've done would be like blaming a slave for his condition. Stuff beyond the slave's control took him over. Not that I claim no responsibility. But I don't claim it all."

She paused, as if waiting for a reply, but I didn't answer. I looked into what was left of the fire. The last log wore a feeble yellow flame.

"Your mama and daddy was slaves."

"Yes," I said. "They were."

"They didn't want to be."

"I reckon not."

"And you don't blame them for it."

"No."

She took a deep breath, seemed to square her shoulders, and looked me in the eye. "But you blame me."

I thought about it. I had the sense I was being taken into uncharted waters where the things I believed in were not as certain as they'd been on the shore I'd left. There were good women and bad women. Bad women were whores. I'd heard stories about whores with hearts of gold, but that's just what they were—stories. I didn't think of whores as women with a past, or reasons for doing what they did. They were simply fixtures who provided to men who could pay for it what those men so desperately needed.

Now Rachel was suggesting that things were more complicated than that. It was not a complication I wanted to unravel. Someone had once told me he'd never met a man who'd been to prison who'd admitted his guilt. Maybe the same was true for whores. Maybe none of them took the blame for what they did.

But was that a good comparison? Whores hadn't broken the law. Or at least they hadn't broken man's law. I dismissed it. It wasn't for me to decide.

"I know my daddy's story," I said. "And my mama's. I don't know yours."

She looked at me with her eyebrows raised.

"You mean I might have *wanted* to be a whore?"

Coming out of her mouth the word seemed more wretched than it was, and I found myself wishing I had another way to say it.

"I mean I don't know."

"That's what I'm telling you," she said. "That I never wanted to." I caught the edge in her voice, and I didn't know why I was surprised that she had some fight in her.

"Everybody's got a story," she said.

"I reckon so."

She leaned back, her arms stretched, head turned toward the sky, deepening the hollow in her throat. "I love Halifax," she said. "That he came along might be the closest I ever come to a miracle." Her arms relaxed, her head came back to her knees, and her eyes were closed. She looked so young, so sad, and I was waiting for her to continue, to ask me that I keep her past to myself, that I protect the love and safety that she'd found. I was thinking there was nothing I could do, that even if I did make a vow of silence, still, people would know. It was beyond my control. Being a whore was not something you could hide. Folks back my way would smell it. This was what I'd been raised to believe. And like everybody else, I was a creature of my upbringing.

As I thought this, I wished it wasn't so. I found myself thinking maybe she was right. Love was rare and deserved to be protected. But I hadn't made the world we lived in, although I would, as God was my helper, keep silent about her past.

I waited for her to ask for my silence, and I would have promised it, but she said instead, "Well, I'm going to say good night." Her voice had a deep, deep sorrow in it, and she made to rise, and I felt something move in me, and I knew it was caring. I was touched by her sadness. And I wanted to be in her company for just a little longer.

"Wait," I said.

She seemed to be suspended in her rising, and I said, "If you want to tell me, I'll listen."

She sat back down and told me.

CHAPTER THIRTEEN

She'd been born in New Orleans in 1848. Her mother was Creole and free, the daughter of a man who worked metal, who built his share of the wrought-iron gates and balconies that graced the city. She'd been taught to read and write and be a lady. She lived alone with her mother, who cleaned for white people during the day.

Both her mother's parents were dead. She had no relatives except her mother's father's sister in Florida. Her mother promised that one day they'd go there, and Rachel would meet the rest of her kin.

Twice a week, in the evening, her mother bathed and dressed and powdered, and left until morning. She knew now that her mother had gone to be with her father, a white man whose name had been kept from her. She'd never been told how her mother and father had met.

Other than her mother's absence during those evenings, it had been a normal childhood. She had friends and moved among people much like her. She learned about love from Alfonse, the man her mother left her with until she was old enough to spend those nights alone. Alfonse loved her mother. He was a gentle man who sometimes came for

dinner, who sometimes sat with her mother in the garden
well into the night, but who was always gone in the morning. He'd taught Rachel by his example the permanence of
genuine love. He was there through all the years of her
childhood, and her mother said to call him uncle.

Alfonse was over six feet tall. When he laughed his body
shook, but the sound of his laughter was quiet. When Rachel understood the reason for his presence, she sought to
discover if Alfonse was in pain from being so close to her
mother without possessing her. Once she asked him, and
he smiled, and said, "Love does not hurt. Remember that."

She was aware of slaves, but had never been taught to
consider their condition. They were part of the natural order
of things, like sky or air.

The war came. Although she knew about it and heard
about it from the grown-ups around her, it had no effect on
her life. She now suspected that the white man who was
her father had served to protect them.

Then the war was over, and her mother went into mourn-
ing. Her father had died. Several months later, her mother
came down with consumption. Alfonse had asked her
mother to move in with him so he could care for her, but
she said it wasn't honorable, that if she hadn't been able to
give herself to him while she was healthy, she wouldn't be
a burden to him now. She wrote to her aunt in Florida, who
lived in a small town named Eatonville, and word came
back to come.

One morning in the milky light of a Louisiana dawn,
Rachel and her mother packed their belongings into a
wagon. Her mother had given in to Alfonse's insistence that
he be the one to go with them to make certain of their
safety.

They headed north, crossed the Louisiana border into
Mississippi, turned east toward Georgia. The route that Al-

fonse had chosen would take them to Lowndes County. Then they'd head south into Florida.

That was the plan for the four-week trek of their journey, but they never arrived. Her mother died in Alabama, just this side of the Georgia border. They buried her beneath a willow on the bank of the Chattahoochee River.

Rachel was slammed into an agony so deep it kept her from crying. Alfonse, wounded by his own grief, tried to console her.

When they reached the town on the evening of the day they'd buried her mother, it was already nightfall. She couldn't remember the town's name. What she did remember was that they couldn't find a place to stay. The man who ran the rooming house didn't like the expression on Alfonse's face when he looked at him, which was merely grief ravaged by disbelief that they were being turned away, and then an awful resignation. They returned to the wagon, rode until they came to the edge of a wood, and they turned off and stopped beneath a tree. They'd eaten a little. She remembered the sound of an owl's mournful hoot, and the rustling in the trees and the fields beyond them. Those sounds hadn't been so frightening when her mother was alive. Her mother had laughed, and held her and said there was nothing to fear.

She lay down in the wagon. Alfonse was beneath it. She'd not thought she'd sleep, but she did. When she awoke it was to the sound of shouting white men on horseback. Two of them held Alfonse and recited a list of his crimes. They included being sassy, moodiness, and the likelihood of further criminal action. Alfonse listened in silence. The white men put him on the back of a horse and tied a rope around his neck. They slung the other end of a rope over a tree limb and wrapped it around the trunk. They slapped the horse and it started forward, and only then did

Alfonse speak, and it was to say, "Sweet Jesus." She would never in her life hear someone say "Jesus" without thinking of the man who so perfectly loved her mother.

They weren't satisfied with hanging Alfonse. They raped her. There were six of them, and they lined up and each took his turn, groaning and spitting, and they left her beneath a tree in the shadow of a hanged man, in a country where she was a stranger, and all the time she was thinking, *Why?* Why were these men, who she didn't know, and had done nothing to inspire their hatred, why were they doing this to her?

The men took what they wanted from the wagon. They took the horse. She dragged her body into the wagon, staring at the star-drunk sky for what was left of the night. After awhile she began to sing a song her mother had taught her as a child, "Oh, Mary, don't you weep," and then she began to pray. She prayed to Jesus and to Mary, to the God of Abraham, to Loa, to the spirits in living things, in rivers and stars, every deity she'd ever heard of she called to. She prayed, not for deliverance, but for the soul of Alfonse, who was gentle and steadfast, and she prayed for the strength to live with the memory of what had happened to her.

Day broke, and she wondered where she would go, what she would do in this strange and violent country. She cringed as she heard the sound of a buggy on the road, curled herself into a knot, and prayed they wouldn't stop to ask why she was there. But who wouldn't have stopped at the sight of a black man hanging from a tree, and a wagon with a young girl curled in a knot?

Three women were in that buggy. It was driven by a bear of a white man who had some Indian in him, a deaf mute named Roscoe, who was going with them to Texas, where men were plenty and white women few. The women planned to make their fortunes selling their bodies to those who had the money to pay. Then they planned to move on toward some unknown future where they'd live together in peace.

All this Rachel learned later. One of the women was Dora, who in two years saved enough to buy the hotel in Laredo. The women bathed her, dressed her in fresh clothes, held her, spoke soothingly, eased her fear and humiliation.

Roscoe cut Alfonse down and they buried him, and stood above the grave and said a prayer, and then they started off to Texas. The two people she'd loved most in the world, the people who'd loved and protected her, she'd left buried in unmarked graves that she could never return to visit.

Rachel went with the women to Laredo, where she'd stayed for six years. She'd told herself that it didn't matter if she was a whore, because her body was already defiled. She would use the weakness in men to get what she wanted, which was enough money so that one day she could leave.

Time passed, and the women's plans changed. Once Dora gave up the idea of leaving Laredo, the rest lost their will to go. But Rachel didn't give up her dream. It was the idea of leaving that made it possible to live.

One day she understood that she had enough money to, but no one except her mother's people in Florida to go to. And she had no desire to go there, to answer questions about what her life was. This discovery nearly paralyzed her. She bent herself to living one day at a time, refused to think about what would happen when her beauty faded.

That was how she was living when Halifax came along, wondering if it was worth her while to head for Florida anyway, wondering if any of her relatives were alive, and if so, would they take her in, and could she hide what she'd done from them?

*   *   *

While she told her tale, the night had clouded. I heard the howl of a coyote way off in the distance, and the fire had burned to its ember. I was empty inside, wanting to rewrite her past, hold and comfort her, find some words that would say what I felt.

All I had was the reaching of my heart, all I could say was, "Rachel, I'm sorry," but when I said it, she didn't answer.

We sat on either side of a dying fire, and I vowed to myself that nothing I said or did would threaten her life with Halifax, that I would defend them, if not by word, then by everlasting silence.

I said it again, "Rachel, I'm sorry," and she answered in a voice that was drained of energy and spirit. "I know," she said.

We sat awhile, and she whispered good night. When she left, she took a part of me with her.

Her tale haunted me. For days it stayed in the front of my mind, moved only by the power of forgetfulness found in work. At night it kept me from sleeping. I'd toss and turn, filling in the details of her story, imagining witnessing it, wondering what such an experience would have done to me. I imagined something like that happening to Amelia, and I hid my face and wept.

The third night, when I couldn't sleep, I got up to walk, my body tired, my mind racing. I headed away from the center of the camp, toward a clump of stunted trees that threw dwarfed shadows from the light of a just-full moon. Suddenly, I was alert. What sounded like the cry of someone wounded had come from the dark before me. I crept forward, and now the silence was as deep as a grave. I'd begun to think I'd imagined the cry, when I heard the voices. I dropped to my knees, inched forward, and when I understood the source of the sounds, I felt silly and ashamed. But I didn't drop my eyes, or go back the way I'd come.

It was Rachel and my brother Halifax. She was on her back with her legs wrapped around him, he moving in her perfect fit, and the full moon lit them. I wanted to move away, but I was afraid I'd make a sound and they'd hear me. I wanted to stay and watch. I knelt, listening to her soft moans, and I watched, and I heard my brother's groaning. I heard Rachel's whisper, and sensed the building, and she said, "yes," and I felt what was happening in my pants. I tore myself from the scene, backed away on all fours in the light of that shining moon.

For the next few days, it was hard to be in Rachel's presence, hard to face her bright smiles, and her display of brotherly affection to me. Whenever I looked at her, I felt the longing in the pit of my stomach, and my flesh would rise. I wondered if I was being unfaithful to Amelia, and tried to substitute Amelia for Rachel in my imagining. I couldn't do it. No matter how hard I tried, it was Rachel who smiled at me, Rachel's teasing tongue, Rachel's face twisted with heat and pleasure.

I needed to pray. I went to a hill beyond the camp. I faced the west where the sun went down like a blood-red promise, and birds swirled in the air, black against the sky. I prayed hard and long, and asked for deliverance. I stopped to rest a while, and when I did, I thought of Rachel.

I knew then what I didn't understand until later, that the strongest bonds are forged when people tell their stories to others who listen. That sorrow and suffering bring us together with a passion resembling love.

I stood up, turned in a circle, looked at the sky. The sky looked back, speechless, uncaring. I fell to my knees again.

I prayed. I prayed that this feeling for my brother's woman would pass from me.

When I finished, I didn't feel any better, but I felt I'd done all I could.

On the eighty-third day of our journey, the beautiful weather vanished. The sky grew black and a hard rain came, and it was impossible to stay dry. For four days the rain fell while the drive inched northward, and we all were so miserable that nobody sang.

Then the rain stopped, the sky cleared.

Bradford hadn't doubled back during the storm, but once it ended, he galloped out of the camp an hour before dusk. He returned just before darkness fell, and came looking for me. His hat was jammed down over his forehead, and his shoulders were hunched, and his face wore a scowl as dark as the just-passed storm.

"There's another herd back there," he said. "Two, maybe three days behind us."

"That a problem?"

"There's two men between us and them."

I was sitting with my back against the wheel of Seth's wagon, feeling just as tired and weary as could be. I had what was left of a cup of lukewarm coffee, and I slugged it empty to the bottom, poured out the grounds, and looked at Bradford. He wasn't looking at me. He was looking back into the darkness toward the direction he'd come from.

"What you think they want?"

"I got no idea. For all I know they could be on their way to Abilene like us."

"They're not with the herd? Lead riders, maybe?"

He shook his head, and Rachel passed by, a bounce in her walk. She turned her lovely face and spoke to us. Bradford grunted. I said hello.

When she was out of hearing, I stood up, rubbed a hand across my chin. "Well, what do we do?"

Bradford shrugged. "Wait. They can travel a whole lot faster than us. If they catch up, we'll see what's going on. If they don't . . ."

"If they don't, what?"

"Something's up."

"Any idea what?"

"One or two."

I waited. When I knew he wasn't going to tell me what those ideas were without my asking, I controlled the hot feeling that rose in me. "How'd they get through the Indians?"

"Indians don't usually bother with a couple of men riding through as long as they mind their business."

"Should we tell the men?"

"No use getting them upset until we know what's going on."

That afternoon, I rode to the top of a bluff, and looked back the way we'd come, but there was no one in the space behind us. I turned and looked at the cattle, who'd moved all day at a good clip. We'd only lost a couple of dozen beyond those we'd given to the Indians. Bradford said that the abundance of food and water, and the reasonable pace we moved at had left the herd in good shape. We could count on top dollar when we got to Abilene. For a moment I wondered if we'd make it, but I pushed that thought aside.

My mind lit on Rachel, and on how my heart had jumped when she smiled. I'd been fighting what she made me feel. I'd told myself it wasn't anything unusual. I was a man who'd been a long time away from his woman, and Rachel was lovely, and had told her story to me. That's all it was. She was my brother's woman, and besides, I loved Amelia. If I hung on, the feeling would go away.

I strained to look through the afternoon, back into the distance. I couldn't see a thing.

In the morning the sun was shining, and we drove toward Abilene. Days before we got to the Red River the weather grew hot and dry, dust everywhere, in my mouth and nose and eyes. Water, when we came to it, was not plentiful. We pushed the cows that had started to become unruly with thirst and heat, and three days later we came to the Red River. When the cows smelled the water, their eyes widened and their nostrils flared, and we couldn't do anything but let them run. They headed toward the river nearly two thousand strong, their hooves like drumbeats on the dry and dusty earth.

We crossed the river in a day. The cows behaved themselves, the horses swam the muddy water with their tails spread like fans behind them. The men hooted and hollered that we were almost through with our journey, and when we reached the other side, they yelled back at the next-to-last river we'd have to cross.

Every night before we bedded down, Bradford reported that the two men were still behind us. They hadn't come any closer.

I swallowed my pride and asked what that meant. Bradford said he didn't know. Maybe bounty hunters. Maybe rustlers. Or maybe just drifters who had no place in particular to go and the rest of their lives to get there.

I kept looking back over my shoulder, but nothing was there, and in a little while the fact that I couldn't see lulled me, and the danger behind us, if danger it was, receded like the horizon.

The drive moved forward, and I knew it was the fact of nearing our destination, but it felt we were moving slower than at any point since we'd left Laredo. The sun that rose in the morning took its own sweet time to cross the sky, and I'd finally fall asleep at night and wake rested, and it would still be three hours to dawn.

But the sun did keep to its appointed journey, and nights did pass, and we moved in a steady, mile-devouring pace. And one bright morning, one hundred and thirteen days after we'd left Laredo, the point man came galloping back into camp and skidded his horse to a stop. He said he'd seen the roofs of Abilene in the distance. I called to the men, and we let out a shout and threw our hats in the air.

Part
THREE

CHAPTER FOURTEEN

Abilene was on the other side of the Smoky Hill River, which was narrow enough to throw a stone across, and shallow enough to wade. The current was slow and lazy. The banks were tame slopes, hard for good footing, and moving the cows would be easy. Bradford had the men hold the herd steady while him and me went to town.

I coaxed my horse into the mud-brown river. The water had a dirty smell. It was warm and littered with garbage. I saw a whiskey bottle float by with the stopper still in its neck. I saw a pair of cowboy's britches, and a worn-out boot looking sad at being abandoned. A film spread on the water, like fried fat or oil for lanterns. It left marks on my boots, and I hoped nothing in it was catching.

It was the middle of the afternoon on a Thursday, and Abilene's one street was full of drunk cowboys and whores. The men waved whiskey bottles, swung the women in dizzying circles, and everything was said in a shout.

The noise was a steady, distant sound. From time to time pistol shots sounded like fireworks on the Fourth of July. There were no children as far as I could see, and when I

looked through the dirty bank window, I saw that business
was brisk.

Facing the muddy river was a line of buildings, some so
recently built I could smell the sap in the wood. The building at the end was a three-story hotel that rose like a brooding, man-made mesa at the end of the dusty street. It was
painted a sickly gray, and it looked like four builders who
didn't agree had been paid to put it together. A huge sign
in black letters at the top said its name was DROVERS COT-
TAGE.

We made our way past the blacksmith and two saloons
and the sheriff's, and an office that said it sold land. Past
that, a brand-new flag above its door, was the United States
Post Office.

"Hold it a minute," I said to Bradford. I slid off my
horse and went inside.

The President was still sitting in judgment. I nodded to
him like an old acquaintance, and I spoke to the postmaster
who was in a jolly mood. He wanted to talk of the long
drive north, the absence of women and whiskey, the feel
of clean sheets after months of the same dirty blanket. He
spoke about the high time I'd have tonight, and for a moment I thought he'd been drinking. I let him go on a little,
then managed to get him to turn his attention to what the
government had hired him to do. He moved to his right
and leafed through a box, and his hand came out with four
letters from Amelia. He wished me luck and a long life,
and something else I didn't hear because I was outside
when he said it.

Bradford was frowning and asking what had took me so
long. I told him I'd run into a man with a gift for gab, and
I'd felt it my place to swap a word, so he wouldn't think
me a savage. Bradford snorted and raised his eyebrows, and
for a minute I thought he would smile.

I put the letters inside my shirt, against my skin. I'd read them later, after a bath in that gray hotel.

Another pistol shot rang out, and a horse hollered, and a cowboy's yell carried above the din, and it spoke of joy and deliverance. I looked at the sky. The sun fell in broad, sharp angles. The clouds were clean white and puffy. The sky was a smoked shade of blue, and a hawk spread its wings against it.

We walked our horses along the street, avoiding the cowboys involved in their celebrations. Behind the hotel was a stretch of land between two sets of railroad tracks and the backs of the buildings. The train station had a roof that looked sat on by a giant. On a ridge that rose behind the station and meandered off to the east, a passel of new houses was being built, and I wondered who would live there. I could hear the distant ringing of driven nails, see the rise and fall of hammers before I heard them, and the men from where I was were hardly the size of children. Then we rode around the side of the hotel, and the sight took my breath away.

It looked like a million cows. Beyond the railroad tracks, to the left of where the houses were going up, were the pens where cattle snorted and shifted and waited to journey east. I had a bad moment. The last time I'd seen this many head together was back in Mexico, at Romero's. I was thinking that if all those cattle were here to be sold, and herds were behind me driving toward Abilene with the same purpose, my prospects for profit might not be as good as I'd thought.

I said this to Bradford, and he said not to worry. There were a whole lot of hungry people back east. Their appetite for beef would hardly be met if we'd managed to collect every last longhorn in Texas.

The cattle smell seemed to be just above us, like a stinking, second sky. We rode toward the building that had steep steps to the office and a brand-new sign that read TOPEKA LIVESTOCK COMPANY. The front of the building had a porch with six steps. It had a railing that said to lean on it was to put your life in its hand.

Bradford asked me what the sign said, and I told him.

"This where we sell the herd?" I asked, and he nodded and allowed that it was.

Halfway to the building, Bradford reined in his horse, and when I turned to see why he'd stopped, his head was cocked to one side.

"Listen," he said.

I listened, but all I heard was the carousing men, and the shriek of a whore, the hammers, and the cattle. I looked at Bradford with my eyebrows up. Then I heard it, although it was more like I felt it, a rumble from the west. And we turned, and in a little while, the train came out of the distance, snorting and singing its mournful song, and smoke black and thick as an Indian signal rose from its brooding face.

"That there's the Kansas Pacific Railroad," Bradford said, and awe was in his voice. We watched until the train stopped, and the engineer blew the whistle that made me shiver, and the cattle raised their heads in sad and stupid wonder. Then we rode up to the building with the sign and the rickety railing.

We had to wait in line while two herders did business before us. When it was our turn, we talked to a man named McCoy, who wore a store-bought suit and blunt-toed Eastern shoes. A silver head of a longhorn was pinned to his right lapel. He had a sharp nose and a beard streaked with gray and hands as slight as a woman's. He was missing a thumb on his left hand, and he didn't bother to hide it. On the desk near that hand was a forty-four with its muzzle aimed at the door. Two cowboys smoking cigarettes and holding shotguns in their lap slouched on chairs in opposite corners.

If McCoy was taken aback that two black men were standing in front of him, negotiating for placing close to two thousand head of Texas cattle, he got over it in a minute. He told us what to do and how to do it.

When I said if he bought horses I had a remuda to sell, he answered that he didn't. But he told me where to go and to speak to a man named Duffy.

"Don't expect to make a killing," McCoy said. "He knows you want to get rid of them, and he's going to take advantage."

I thanked him for his advice. We rode back out the way we'd come and crossed the filthy river. We talked to the men. They were eager to be done and paid for their trouble. Some were staring across the river at Abilene. They looked like thirst-crazed cattle down wind from water's sweet smell.

We circled the herd and drove them through the shallow river, and, like I'd thought, it was easy. Halifax stopped at the hotel to get a room for him and Rachel, and I told him to sign up me and Bradford and Grafton. When we reached the stockyards, a pen was ready for us, and we got the cattle inside. Two men sat on the pen gate and counted. The cattle were shuffling, and smelled to high heaven, and their horns clicked when they met.

The counting and weighing were done before dark, and the cowboys stood around expectant. Bradford and I went inside to take care of the final business. When we'd finished I'd sold 1,959 cattle at $25 a head for a total of $48,975. I made myself stay calm, like I was used to being in the presence of all that money. The man with the missing thumb gave me $5,000 in cash and the rest in a banknote. He said the bank would stay open till late.

"I'd rather have all cash," I said.

He looked up at me, eyebrows raised.

"I don't want to run into any trouble with a bank wanting to know how a colored man come to have a banknote in this amount."

McCoy gave me an understanding smile. "Won't be no trouble," he said. "Least not in Abilene. If there is, come see me. I'm here till way past midnight, and I'll be right back here at dawn."

I thanked him and took the money and the banknote. I sent Halifax and Grafton to find the man who bought horses. I told them to take any reasonable price, but not to give them away. I rode to the bank next to Bradford, and the cowboys were like shadows behind us.

The bank business took a few minutes, and when it was finished I had two saddlebags of cash. I paid Bradford inside, at a table near a dirty window. When Bradford tried to give me the twenty dollars I'd advanced him, I told him to take it as a bonus.

We came outside, and I paid off the hands. I told Esteban, Romero's man, that I'd give him Romero's money in the morning. Esteban nodded. He looked like something was bothering him, but when I asked, he shrugged.

We shook hands all around and the men scooted into the coming night, disappearing into the darkness and the knots of cowboys that filled the town's one street. Some said so long, and some didn't.

I had a funny moment. I felt like we'd come to the close of something important, and the finish had left me empty. I wondered if Bradford felt it too, and I started to ask him, but something told me not to. I shook my head to clear it of the feeling, and turned to Bradford, and I made my face show nothing.

"Well," I said. "We did it."

My voice sounded deeper than I was used to hearing it, and for whatever reason, I swallowed. Bradford said the fact was that we had.

I stuck my hand out and he shook it, and that was the end of it all.

We headed to the hotel. We'd meet for supper in an hour. At the hotel desk I gave the clerk my saddlebags to put in the hotel safe. I told the clerk we wanted bath water in our rooms. I asked him for something to write with, and he gave me a pencil that was chewed near the tip and two sheets of wrinkled paper.

I put the pencil and the folded paper in my pocket, and we ordered a drink at the bar. The whiskey went down hard and bit the back of my throat and left a slow warm in my stomach. It was good, but not as good as I'd dreamed. We had another drink, and then went our separate ways.

My room looked out on the cow pens and the new houses going up on the ridge and the purple evening falling hard above it. Someone had poured water in the tub, but when I put my hand in, it was still too hot for sitting.

I flopped across the bed and wondered why I felt lonely. I touched the letters from Amelia that I'd stuck inside my shirt. I decided I'd read them later. I felt my spirits sinking. We'd made a profit of $40,000 and I felt like a man in a poorhouse.

Why didn't I feel better, now that my dream was about to come true? I turned and twisted the question, but I couldn't come up with an answer.

I walked across the room, and the bath was ready to sit in. I took off my clothes. I put Amelia's letters on the floor next to the tub and stepped into the healing water.

For a while I just soaked. Then I picked up Amelia's letters and read them.

She still loved me. The summer was hot and dry. Not a day passed that she didn't pray for me, and she hoped I'd kept *my* promise to pray. My description of the Texas countryside that I'd wrote in my letters made her think of the glory of God.

That was the first letter. The next three were much the same, except in one she reported trouble at several farms south and east of my family's. Twice, bands of marauding white men had come from the south and stopped to harass small farmers. Fortunately, nothing serious had happened. A haystack had been burned in a neighboring county. At another farm, livestock had been shot and left in the fields to rot.

I put the letters on the floor, away from the tub, so I wouldn't get water on them. I pulled my knees to my chest and fought the empty feeling.

I started thinking about the past few months, how this undertaking had been marked by strife and killing. The hanged rustlers, a dead sheriff, Steele and his band of thieves. And I'd taken part in that, and I wondered if it had changed me, and if that was why I was blue. Even though I hadn't taken anyone's life, I'd been present, and so I was part of it all.

And I'd broken the law by breaking Halifax out of jail— that was as clear as drinking water. I'd been raised to believe there were always consequences for my actions, good or bad. I wondered what price I'd pay.

Then I understood that the feeling that had me in its grip came from waiting for my punishment. I just didn't know when it would come and what form it would take, and that's what had me on edge.

I had good reason to be on edge. I could end up in jail, or hanged by my neck from a tree. I could get sick with some strange disease. I could go through life carrying the weight of guilt and expectation, looking over my shoulder, waiting for the punishment.

Then it hit me, and I grunted, surprised and dismayed at the thought. Of all the consequences available, the only one that caused real worry was Amelia's finding out.

But I had promised myself that Amelia never would.

If I was sure she wouldn't, then why was I so worried?

I thought about that for a while and decided that I was less worried about Amelia learning what I'd done than having to live a lie. How could I have a life with someone if I was living a lie?

The truth was I was already doing it. I'd started the day I took Caesar's advice to never tell about shooting that young white drifter. I'd never even told my brothers.

I cupped my hands together and lowered them into the tub and brought them up to pour water on my face. I wished I'd brought whiskey to my room. I had the feeling that a couple more drinks would soothe me. Then I thought that maybe prayer would help, and at the idea something rose up hard inside me.

What was this resistance? It had started before the killing, well before. Two weeks away from Amelia and my daily prayer had ceased to mark my evenings.

Then I thought how this kind of thinking had moved to the back of my mind during the last weeks of the drive. I realized I'd enjoyed a stretch when I'd been released from the sense that whatever would happen would end up being the worst. Looking back, the only way I could describe it was to say that I'd been free. I wondered if that freedom came from a clear-cut purpose, and work so hard it brought peace. Or was it just another kind of human failing, a convenient forgetting, for which, along with my other misdeeds, I'd end up having to pay?

I thought back to the country we'd crossed, the wideopen spaces, a sky that made me feel tiny and insignificant, the mile-long trail of cattle. Maybe I had stopped praying, but I still had questions about God. My guess was that God was indifferent, too busy doing whatever God does to be concerned with me. And if God didn't care, then fate and chance didn't give a hoot about me either.

No, I concluded, if I was to be punished, God would have nothing to do with it. I didn't need to worry about chance any more than the next man did. The law of Texas was one hundred thirteen days behind me, and I resolved not to punish myself. Only Amelia seemed capable of calling me to task, of judging me, or, more important, only she seemed interested in doing so.

I felt a twinge of annoyance. Amelia had no right to be more exacting than God.

I got out of the tub, dried myself, shook dust from my clothes. I thought I saw movement through my window. When I went to look outside, two men with their heads bent toward one another stood in conversation. One had a dirty white hat, and while I watched, he took it off and wiped his forehead.

I dressed and went to meet the others. I left my Winchester in the room, but I wore my pistol to supper.

CHAPTER FIFTEEN

When I got downstairs, the others were sitting in the room's far corner, away from the carousing at the bar. The room was thick with cowboys and whores, the ceiling was low, and the tables round and wooden. Lamps burned slow on the walls and their light was soft and yellow. As I walked toward Bradford and my brothers, a lawman came to the hotel's swinging doors, stepped inside, and scanned the room with careful, hawklike eyes. He stood a while, then turned and went outside.

Rachel looked like a dream, wearing a pale blue dress, hair piled on top of her head. I asked where she'd gotten such a pretty thing in this godforsaken town, and she laughed and said she'd brought it with her.

Halifax looked as happy as he could be. Grafton was leaning back in his chair, holding a glass of whiskey and wearing a contented look. The lines in Bradford's forehead had eased, his eyes were easy, and his face looked ready to smile.

Being in the presence of my brothers and Rachel and Bradford made me feel better, eased the weight I'd felt upstairs in my room. Nobody talked much. I guessed they were feeling what I'd begun to feel, satisfaction that a long, hard task was completed, a little awed that we'd done it.

I told my brothers what was in Amelia's letters. They asked a couple of questions about folks back home, and then we grew quiet again. The waitress brought another bottle of whiskey and set it in front of Bradford. She was a hefty woman with a gap between her front teeth, and a smile that lit up her face. She and Bradford looked at each other for longer than a moment. When she left, Halifax tried to tease Bradford about the look the two had exchanged. But the teasing had no energy in it, and Bradford just looked at Halifax as if he was speaking French.

We got quiet again, but it was comfortable. I looked around the room and saw some of our cowhands having themselves a grand old time. A couple were drunk already. I saw Esteban, one of the Mexicans that Romero had sent with us, standing at the bar. He was holding a glass of whiskey, but he looked worried and alone. I went over to the bar, and invited him to sit with us. Some of the cowboys looked at me hard, as if to say it was bad enough to have colored men in their midst, and now here was a Mexican. But most were too drunk to notice, and some were too drunk to care.

When I asked Esteban why he looked so troubled, he said he was worried about going back to Mexico by himself and having to be responsible for Romero's money. It seemed like a reasonable concern. It was a long way back to the Rio Grande. A lot of bad things could happen to a lone Mexican carrying a saddlebag full of money.

"What you think, Bradford?" I asked. "Does it make sense to pay a couple of hands to go with him?"

"Who do you know you can trust?" Bradford said.

"What about wiring it?" Grafton said. "Esteban can pick it up in Mexico."

Bradford shook his head. "Romero's nowhere near a town. It we send it to Laredo, people will be suspicious about a Mexican picking up all that money, and they'll figure out he was riding with us. We're wanted men in Laredo, and they wouldn't need much excuse to throw Esteban in jail."

Bradford shook his head, picked up his glass and drained it. He set the glass on the table, and the light shined on it. He wiped his mouth with his hand. "What we should've done," he said, "was to get a letter from Romero saying that Esteban was his man, and carrying his money." He thought about what he'd said. "I don't know. Even that might not have worked. Somebody going to rob Esteban here wouldn't wait politely while he fished out a letter. They'd shoot and steal first, then find out they was in a heap of trouble with the toughest *hombre* south of the border."

I was thinking of Petey, who'd been one of the men who laid the false trail for Steele's men and who hadn't come back from the mission. We hadn't figured that something would happen to Petey who was supposed to ride with Esteban.

I said, "What if we send the money to Laredo in Romero's name?"

"How do we get word to him?" Halifax asked.

"Send Esteban back to tell him."

"That might work," Bradford said, and waved his arm. The waitress came over. Bradford asked her what was good, and she said not to take a chance on anything but the steak. So that's what all of us ordered. Steak and red wine, and soft-cooked white potatoes, and it was good and the way I liked it. I had a bad moment when Grafton wryly wondered if we were eating one of our own cows. Rachel told him to behave himself, and all of us laughed.

Dinner was slow and easy. When we'd finished, we sat over wine, and Bradford toasted us and our journey. He said it in English and in Spanish, so as to include Esteban, and I was thinking about asking Bradford to fill in the details of how he'd learned to speak Spanish, when the crack of a pistol seemed to be fired in my ear. I turned toward the sound and reached for my gun all in the same motion, and Halifax was ducking, and Grafton was wearing a puzzled look, and Rachel's head exploded in a shower of bone and blood.

I'll never be able to say exactly how it happened. My mind had gotten instantly clear, but it was noting the strangest things. First was the pattern of Rachel's blood on the walls, the way her head was thrown back at a silly angle. At the same time, I was hearing the sudden lull in the noise in the bar, and then the swelling of sound and movement. People were scurrying for cover, the screams of women stabbed the air, and the sound of gunfire was rapid.

I dove for the floor as Bradford turned the table over, throwing dishes and glasses and steak bones, and Grafton and Halifax were diving on either side of it, and I heard the sounds of bullets as they splintered the wooden shield.

I rolled twice, three times, away from the table, my gun drawn, and I remember the boots of a cowboy that had a scuff on the toe and heels that needed replacing. I rolled again and the room was deafening with gunfire, and when I was on my stomach, gun pointed in the direction from which the first shot had come, I saw a man in a dirty white hat who was crouched and shooting steady. To his right, behind a column that barely protected his body, squatted another man, bare-headed, with a day-old beard and his gun aimed point-blank at Bradford. Bradford squeezed off two shots, and the bare-headed man fell, and I started rapid firing at the man in the dirty hat. I must have hit him three or four times and he looked surprised and went backwards, and suddenly the room was quiet.

"Halifax," I shouted. "Grafton."

"We're okay," Grafton said.

I stood up, carefully. Bradford was turning in a circle, his gun at the ready. I looked around the room. People stood as if frozen, the good feeling of whiskey driven away. Two whores had hands at their mouths, and another was sobbing in the thick arms of a cowboy whose eyes were closed. The man behind the bar was shaking his head and holding a rifle in a way that said he didn't want to use it, but he would.

I looked at the floor. Rachel was lying in a pool of blood that stained her dress the color of wine. One leg was bent beneath her, the other had no shoe. What was left of her face was turned from me.

I heard Halifax make a growling sound on my left. He was holding his gun in one hand. His face was twisted. He was breathing in short shallow breaths that made me think of counting, and he crawled toward the body of his faceless love. He was no more than ten feet from her, but halfway there he stopped as if the effort had worn him out.

Grafton stood up and started to touch him, then pulled his hand away. Halifax resumed his crawling and now, instead of the weird breathing, he was whimpering, and every eye in the room was on him.

The sound Halifax was making went through me like an ice-cold knife. I'd never heard a human make a sound like that. I watched as he put his head on Rachel's stomach and his shoulders began to heave, and I wasn't feeling anything now, just watching. I remember thinking that whatever I was going to feel would come later, if later itself was to come.

I went to my knees, using a table as shelter, and I looked

at Bradford. In my eyes was a question of whether there were any others, and he nodded, and each of us took a long, slow look around the room, and when I turned back to Bradford, his face said it was over.

I got to my feet, and my legs were unsteady. The lawman came through the door. He had a huge Adam's apple and small eyes blacker than coal. As he walked toward us, I heard the sounds his boots made when he stepped on broken glass. His shirt was white, and his boots were shining. Neither of his deputies was old enough to shave. They were nervous and trying not to show it.

The people had started to crowd in on us and the lawman snarled and waved them back, and the room was quiet except for Halifax's whimpers. The lawman looked at my brother a long, hard moment. He turned away, bent over one of the dead men. He stood and went to look at the bushwacker that Bradford had shot. The lawman shook his head and held his chin in his hand.

He turned abruptly back to Halifax. "Make him stop that," he barked, and I said, "Halifax," as hard and mean as I could, and Halifax didn't look at me, didn't move his face from Rachel's blood-soaked belly, but he stopped his whimpering.

The lawman moved off to his right, and that's when I learned they'd got Esteban. He was lying face down. I got close enough to see the two holes in the back of his head before the lawman told me to move. The lawman reached down and pulled something out of the bare-headed man's shirt. It took him a while to read it. When he'd finished, he handed it to me.

I read it and felt my stomach drop. It was a wanted poster, dead or alive, for the Partlow brothers and Bradford. The poster said we'd killed a lawman and broken a murderer out of jail. The reward was one thousand dollars. I handed the poster to Grafton.

"Fellows got yourself into a bit of trouble in Laredo," the lawman said. If his voice was any quieter I'd have sworn he didn't care.

"Bounty hunters?" I asked.

The lawman nodded.

"It wasn't like that at all," I said.

The lawman looked at me as if to say he wasn't holding his breath until I said I was guilty.

I heard a moan behind me and when I looked Halifax still had his head on Rachel's belly. I thought he was going to start that whimpering again, but he didn't.

I looked at Bradford. He was watching the lawman with the steadiness of a coiled snake.

"Ain't none of my concern whatever you done in Laredo," the lawman said, and it was only then that I knew Bradford had been holding his breath. "But you done created a mess for me. You drive a herd north?"

I nodded.

"You got business at the bank?"

I shook my head. "We finished that."

"Good," he said. "First thing in the morning, let your presence be a memory. Be gone 'fore the sun gets high."

I said we would. The lawman pointed to his deputies, said something, and they bent to grasp the bodies of the bounty hunters. They dragged them toward the door. One of them held his head as if the body smelled, or he didn't want to look into a dead man's open eyes.

The lawman pointed to Esteban and Rachel. "You're responsible for burying your own," he said.

I asked if Abilene had an undertaker, and he laughed and shook his head. "Graveyard's on the other side of town. You'll find shovels in a shed. Lanterns too. Now let's get this mess cleaned up.'' He turned and walked away.

I swear nobody was moving in that room, cutthroat drifter and cowboy, whore and bartender, all as still as the dead of a windless night. They were watching us like we were actors in a play, the final act of which was about to be unfolding.

I took a deep breath and let it out. I looked at Bradford and what I saw in his face let me know it was my call. I had to take care of things from now on.

"Let's go," I said. "We've got to bury the dead."

"Halifax," I said, "get up. Now."

He rose to his feet like a drunk man. His face was covered with blood.

"Pick up Rachel," I said. "Follow me."

I turned to Grafton. "You and Bradford get Esteban."

I turned back to Halifax to see if he was doing what I'd said. He was standing stock still, and his eyes were staring wide. The grief had gone from his face. It was replaced by a mask that looked like stone. He'd cut himself off from his feelings. I hoped it would last until we'd done what we had to.

"Let's go, Halifax," I said. "Pick up Rachel. Come on."

He bent, straightened, then carried her in his arms. Her head was in the curve of his throat. She looked like she was sleeping or overcome by drink. Grafton and Bradford had Esteban between them. Grafton held him under the shoulders and Bradford had his feet.

I turned and went for the door, pushed past it to the lukewarm Kansas night. The street was full of people having themselves a good time. When they saw Halifax with Rachel in his arms, they stared, and the closest ones to us grew quiet.

I stepped into the street and started for the graveyard. The crowds were thick, and they parted to let us through.

I walked slow, with my head up, and my hand was close to my gun. I looked behind me and Halifax was carrying Rachel, and behind him, Grafton and Bradford with Esteban. I walked some more, and when I looked again, some of the cowboys and a few of the whores were following us. Two men were carrying posts of burning wood, and another held a lantern, and the light was flickering in the night.

The graveyard was full of rocks and crude wooden crosses that were white and made by hand. I saw the young deputies across the way digging graves for the bounty hunters while the lawman held a lantern, and I was thinking that I'd remember this night as a festival of death. I'd remember fresh-dug, lonely graves, and whores and drunken cowboys gathering silent, and white handmade crosses that were ghostlike in the dark.

When I got to a spot that had no cross, I stopped. I looked around and saw the wooden shed where the lawman had said it would be. Inside were three good shovels. I brought them back and gave one to Grafton and one to Bradford. The men with the burning wood came close to give us light, and so did the man with the lantern.

We began to dig. The ground was hard and unforgiving, and digging was hard, but we did it, and the folks who'd followed us from the hotel numbered about twenty, and they stood silent while we dug.

I don't know what brought them to participate in our burial. I'd thought it was curiosity, but they were silent in a way the simply curious never are. Maybe it had to do with the violent death of a woman, or the different colors of our skins.

When the graves were finished, we delivered Esteban into the earth. I thought we were going to have trouble with Halifax, that he wasn't going to let Rachel go, but when I spoke to him, he moved forward and let her body down.

We began to cover our friends. The first shovel of dirt hit dead flesh with a sound that was a curse against the living.

We finished, and I was trying to think what to do. I stepped forward, began to recite the Lord's Prayer. For a while it was only my voice, raised in a prayer that brought with it no resistance, and then the people who'd gathered said it with me. I said, "Ashes to ashes, dust to dust," and I looked at the sky. It was black and clouded, and I only saw one star.

I turned to the collected people.

"It's over," I said.

They stood for a moment, as if something I couldn't name had connected them all, and they didn't want to break it. Then they moved off into the night.

"Grafton," I said, "don't let your brother out of your sight."

"Bradford," I said, "we'll meet at sunup downstairs in the hotel."

I turned and left them. I walked back to the hotel by myself. All along the street our funeral procession had only temporarily suspended the celebrations, and everything I heard and saw around me said that death had been forgotten. I went inside the hotel, and people looked at me. I ordered a bottle of whiskey from the bar. I took it upstairs, poured myself a drink, and sat down on the bed.

Rachel was dead, and I didn't know if my brother would recover. I didn't know if I would recover. All during the last weeks of the drive, I'd told myself to let it ride, that time would answer the questions of what I felt for her. Now there was no time. All that loveliness was gone.

I shut my eyes, squeezed them, and then I gave in to the grief and let the tears flow. I was crying for Rachel and for my brother, and I was crying for me, who'd always tried to do right and life just wouldn't permit.

When I'd finished, I dried my face, stopped feeling sorry for myself, and tried to think clearly. Rachel had carried my confusion with her to the grave. And I'd deliberately killed a man because not to be deliberate would have meant my death and the death of my brothers. There was no re-action in me, not at the thought, not at having done it. No blood-red wall behind my eyes, no sinking stomach, no dizziness that said I'd pass out if I moved.

I threw back the drink and poured another.

I wondered if the change in me was permanent. I looked around the room, at the ceiling, the corners, the bottom of my whiskey glass, my heart. I thought of Amelia. Here were more things I couldn't tell her. Would she understand about Rachel if she knew? Would she forgive me for killing when I'd had to? I rubbed a hand across my face, realizing that Amelia's response no longer seemed as important as my own. Who was I, what had I become, and how would it play out in the days I had left on the earth?

And if all that wasn't enough to deal with, Esteban was dead, and I had to figure out how to get Romero's money back to him before he sent someone to keep his promise.

I wanted only one thing at that moment, to shut out the world. I poured another whiskey and tried to drink myself to sleep, but my stomach got sour before I could do it.

CHAPTER SIXTEEN

I was wide awake when morning came to my window. It seemed to show up from a sense of duty, too halfhearted to enter my room.

I grunted and rolled from bed. My stomach was feeling awful. My body complained of soreness and stiffness, and the skin on my face was dry. I needed to wash, but I didn't have any water. I stepped to the window and looked outside, and the town was draped in fog.

I took my time dressing and went downstairs. The room was so empty it felt abandoned. The shutters were open. Someone had righted the tables and chairs and scrubbed the floor. You couldn't tell that four people had died or that the washed-out stains were blood.

The sour rolled in my stomach. I had the feeling that if I closed my eyes the night would rise before me. It would unfold in slow motion in the worn-out light, and there wouldn't be any sound.

A bartender came through the kitchen doors, and his entrance left them swinging. I smelled cooking bacon. The bartender was a big man, with a neck the size of my leg. He wore a derby hat and a handlebar mustache.

I thought about eating, but my stomach decided against it. I ordered coffee. It came in a metal cup and was strong and hot and bracing. I drank it and went outside.

The day still wore the shifting, dead-skinned fog. Bradford and Grafton were in front of the hotel, Bradford next to a saddled black horse with a white diamond in its forehead. I said good morning, and asked Grafton where was his brother.

"Walked over to the graveyard."

"By himself?"

"Yeah."

"I told you not to leave him."

Grafton looked at me, and I heard the sharpness of what I'd said. I didn't try to change it. Grafton turned to Bradford, and stuck out his hand. "So long," he said. "Good luck to you."

He spun and headed toward the graveyard. The fog was like a shroud. I watched as he disappeared.

I said to Bradford, "Heading out?"

"Yeah," he said. "Back to Nebraska. Look in on my people. Then figure out what's next."

For a moment I felt so empty I didn't know what to do.

"Where 'bouts in Nebraska?"

"Weeping Water. Day's ride south of Omaha. Everybody knows the Chilworths."

"Well, if I get up that way, I'll be sure to look you up."

He nodded. "If I'm there, I'll be glad to see you."

"Take care of yourself," I said, and he promised to do what he could. Then he hoisted himself to the back of his horse, raised his hand in salute and rode off.

I watched until he vanished in the fog's mouth. I lifted my face and found the sun's frail outline on the other side of the river. Cow smells, dung and hide and feed, pushed in from the pens behind the buildings. All of it collected, thick and damp, like a weight above my head. The weight made its way to my stomach and riled up the sour again.

I took a last look in the direction Bradford had headed. I thought of what we'd been through, and how he'd got me so mad I'd deliberately hurt his feelings. I wondered why it was it so hard for me to say good-bye and so easy for everyone else.

The fog was retreating before the steadily rising sun. For a moment I had the feeling that the next step taken, or not taken, had no meaning, that everything that had happened was for some purpose it wasn't for me to know.

I walked to the river, stood and watched its sluggish flow. Way on the other side, at the top of a slight incline, the fog rushed to meet the sun, and I could see the lead cows of a herd making its way to Abilene. Distance shrunk the cows to tiny. The mix of fog and sunlight made them dance.

I headed to the train station. The attendant was asleep behind the bars of the ticket booth, his head in the circle of his arms. I spoke to him gently, and he came awake blinking and wiped his mouth with his sleeve.

I told him I wanted three one-way tickets to the closest I could get to Springfield, Missouri, and asked when the next train was due. He said at nine-fifteen in the morning. He pulled a watch from his vest pocket. That would be one hour thirty-seven minutes from now. He said the closest I could get was Jefferson City. The trip was a little better than four hundred miles and we'd lay over in Kansas City. The next train through after this one was three days from now, on Monday.

I bought three tickets and went outside. The sun was big and round and yellow as if it had fed on the fog. The morning wasn't hot yet, but it would be. When I got around to the other side of the buildings, the street was coming alive.

Store owners were throwing back their doors. Still-drunk cowboys paused to look at the sky as if it was something new. I squinted across the river and made out a couple of riders who drove the approaching herd. The lead cows had picked up some size and no longer danced in the light.

I saw Grafton and Halifax coming toward me. Halifax look haunted. His eyes were at the bottom of deep hollows, and his face was gray. I started to ask him if he was all right, but I knew the answer. What I didn't know was if he'd ever be.

I told my brothers we'd be on a train to Jefferson City at a quarter after nine. I told them it might be a good idea to stay inside until it was time to go. I asked what rooms they were in, and I told them the number of mine.

Halifax never even blinked while I spoke. Grafton kept looking like he knew me from somewhere but hadn't been able to place me.

I went back to the hotel. The bartender was eating his breakfast at the bar. He still had on his derby hat, and his chewing was slow and thorough. I told him to have a basin of water sent to my room.

He'd had some home training. He didn't answer until he'd swallowed. Then he asked what room I was in, and I told him.

I went upstairs, flopped across my bed, and tried to look on the bright side. I'd done what I'd set out to do. I'd met some good men, I'd tested myself and so had my brothers, and I believed it had made us stronger.

The other side was that I'd changed, and the way Grafton looked at me said it probably wasn't for the better. Grafton seemed okay, but I really had no way of telling. Halifax I was sure of. He walked and looked like something inside of him had been permanently broken.

A soft knock sounded at the door, and I told whoever it

was to come in. It was the plump waitress with the space between her teeth who'd taken a fancy to Bradford. She looked scared and unhappy, like being in my presence was unlucky. She placed the basin of water and a towel on the chair near the window, and I could see the steam from the water. She didn't look at me. She didn't speak, and I didn't say anything either.

When she left I took off my shirt, undid my gunbelt and washed my face. I poured water over my head and splashed it on my chest. I dried off and flopped across the bed again. I tried to shut down my thinking by listening to the morning. I could hear horses and wagons moving in the street, and the cattle lowing in the pens beyond my room. The men had gone to work on the houses on the ridge, and their hammers were ringing, and now and then a shout rang out that made me think of joy.

I stared out the window, listening to sounds I couldn't see. I had the feeling that my own self was a stranger. I hadn't felt that way since I was a kid, when I was delirious with fever. The fever made my hands and head seem bigger than they were.

The room had grown warmer. I blinked and the delirious feeling left me. I felt sweat in the hollow of my throat. I got a little nervous because I didn't have a watch, and I got up and gathered my belongings. I put my shirt on, and strapped my gun to my waist. I grabbed my Winchester and went down the hall, looking for my brothers. Their rooms were next to one another. I knocked on each, and called out that I'd meet them at the station, and I'd settle the hotel bill.

Downstairs, I got the saddlebags from the hotel safe. I paid the bill and went to the station in the burning morning sun. The station held a little of last night's cool. I sat on a bench against a rough wall, pulled my hat down to the bridge of my nose and stretched my legs. My brothers came in and sat against the opposite wall. Grafton had his eyes closed. Halifax found something to study in the ceiling. I gave one of the saddlebags to Grafton, and kept the other one myself.

The lawman came in, looked at us, and nodded in approval. He left, and we sat awhile, and the room was losing its cool, and the train snorted into the station. We got on and sat in an empty car.

"I got seventy-five dollars for the horses," Grafton said.

I told him he'd done real good. The train pulled out. The conductor took our tickets. I leaned against the train seat and hoped to God I'd sleep.

But I didn't sleep. I looked out the window, and I checked now and then on Halifax. He kept sighing and rubbing his face in his hands. I closed my eyes. I started to think about what had happened, but I stopped and made a pact to myself. I wouldn't think about it anymore until I got home, where I'd have time and space to consider.

Each time the train stopped, people got on. Some looked like businessmen, with Eastern suits. There were a couple of cowboys, and now and then a farmer and his family, looking startled. One of the families had a baby that started to cry, but before I could get annoyed it stopped.

Night fell, and I slept as best as I could with the saddlebag of money between me and the train wall. Once I woke and the night beyond the window was so black I couldn't see. The train wheels beat steady on the track, and I let the rhythms take me back to sleep.

We rode all through the next day and into the night and we came to Kansas City. Halifax and Grafton got off the train to get us something to eat. I stayed put, with the money.

The train pulled out of Kansas City at seven in the morning, and we rode all day and through the night and got to Jefferson City at four the next afternoon. Being on a train all that time made walking on earth seem strange. It took a while to get my legs back, but I was fine by the time we left the station.

After the endless plains of Texas and the one street of Abilene, Jefferson City felt like another world. I'd forgotten how noisy and crowded a city could be. All of it jangled my nerves and made me want to leave as soon as I could.

We stopped to eat in a low-ceilinged room where all the help were men. We bought food supplies for our journey. We got directions to a stable where we purchased three horses and saddles for what Grafton had sold the entire remuda for back in Abilene.

We were a five days' ride from Springfield. For the first hour out of Jefferson City, the road was thick with travelers on their way to the city, some on horseback, some in wagons, some on foot. As we moved farther south, the traffic eased, and as the afternoon wore on there was a stretch when we had the whole road to ourselves.

We rode steadily, the shadows lengthened, the day wound down. The first night we camped beneath the stars, the next night a farmer let us use his barn. The third night we stayed in a hotel in a little town twenty minutes off the road. It was clean and quiet and we were the only ones there.

The morning of the fourth day was cloudy and hot, and I was ready to be done with my journey. So were my brothers. We pushed our horses all day long, we pushed each other. In the fields farmers looked up as we passed and waved.

Just before dark, when the farms had ended for a while, and trees and deep brush lined both sides of the road, a group of men approached us, riding hard. When they got closer, I saw they were white men. The lead rider was a burly chap who was pushing the biggest horse I'd ever seen, maybe seventeen or eighteen hands. The men kept their eyes averted when they passed. Halifax kept riding, but Grafton and I stopped when they'd passed and looked behind us.

"You ever see a horse that size?" I asked.

"I didn't know they came that big," Grafton answered.

"We need to think about bedding down for the night," I said.

He looked up at the darkening sky. "I'll catch up to Halifax, and tell him."

He rode off to fetch our brother, and I was thinking how normal our conversation had been, just two men talking about a horse of improbable size, and the need to stop for the evening. It felt like a long time since we'd talked that way.

I kicked my horse and caught up to my brothers. We turned off into the woods, dismounted, and walked our horses. Fifty yards from the road, we found a clearing with grass for the horses, and a fine little stream of water.

We ate the cold dinner we'd bought from the hotel. Deep in the woods behind us, a hooting owl called. Something small thrashed in the brush, and the stream made a whispering noise, and all the sounds were familiar.

When we'd finished I wrapped the leftover food. We cleaned up the site and washed our faces in the brook.

Halifax spoke for the first time since Abilene. "I'm taking a walk," he said.

We watched him go off into the darkness. Clouds hid the moon and the stars, but the night was warm and pleasant. For a while I sat, waiting to see if Grafton wanted to talk, but when he didn't, I let my mind wander. Before I knew it I was reliving all the killing. How it had started when Steele killed that cowboy who he didn't have to, and how I'd busted Steele's hands up. I thought of the rustlers who'd been shot back in Mexico, and how I'd aimed above their heads, and I thought of Petey who hadn't come back from laying the false trail for the men behind us. There was the cowboy who Halifax had shot in self-defense and the sheriff, and Steele's men trapped by the walls of a sun-drenched canyon, wiped out by Indians whose memory was long. And the bounty hunters who'd rose up out of the crowd shooting to kill while we ate a peaceful dinner, and Rachel, and Esteban, and the bounty hunters themselves who'd got more than they'd bargained for.

Finally, I'd fired to kill rather than wound, and although I'd had a good reason, mainly my need to go on living. Still, I'd done it.

The path behind me was strewn with bodies, and it seemed that was just the way life was, you couldn't avoid violent death. It was a land where men carried guns, and looked for reasons to use them. My hesitation about killing made me unusual, and it was only a little less than a miracle that the hesitation had not cost me my life.

I thought of the beginning of it all, the boy I'd shot, myself no more than a boy, and how that event had shaped me. And I realized that my feeling that the source of my punishment would be Amelia had nothing to do with her. It was me. I wanted to confess to her, I wanted some other breathing, living thing in the world to know what I'd done. But to tell her would mean that she'd reject me and cause the end of my dream. I knew this as certainly as I knew that the sun would rise in the morning, that men would continue to kill one another, that if you wanted to have a life worth living, you had to carve it out of a wilderness of violence and death. You had to be strong, or the world would grind you to dust.

I'd be strong. I wouldn't tell Amelia, but I had to let someone know. I couldn't go through the rest of my life carrying this burden alone.

I remembered Caesar's warning, that I was never to tell anyone that I'd accidently shot that boy. He'd said that the need to tell came from the need to be forgiven, and when it came down strong on me, I had to fight it, take a drink, or find a woman, anything but tell.

Had Caesar meant that I couldn't be forgiven?

I couldn't live alone with it anymore. And so I told Grafton. Told him in the clearing, in the dark, and he listened without so much as a word until I'd finished.

"Damn," he said. "You been carrying that around with you all this time?"

I said I had.

"And blaming yourself?"

"Yes."

I couldn't see his eyes in the darkness, only the mass of his head. Then he said what Caesar had said. "It was an accident. And you were a kid."

I said I knew that.

"I'm glad you told me," he said. "But don't tell no one else. Especially Amelia. Ain't no point in it. I understand the need to have someone else know. You got that now. I'm the one. Let's leave it at that."

"Grafton?"

"Yeah?"

"You think I've changed?"

"I do," Grafton said. "But there's reason for it."

"Is it for better? Or for worse?"

"Neither. It's just change, that's all."

Halifax came back from wherever it was he'd gone. He

didn't say anything, just undid his bedroll, and stretched out on the ground.

"Let's get some sleep," Grafton said.

I said okay, pulled my blanket to my chin. I stretched out in the darkness, feeling as close to peace as I'd felt in a while. I closed my eyes, and slept deep until morning.

CHAPTER SEVENTEEN

At dawn we ate and got back on the road. The sun rose in a ball of fire. Birds were singing to beat the band, and the morning was clear and fine.

The closer I got to home, the more I felt the excitement. I'd see the people I loved. They'd be proud that I'd done what I'd said. I'd gone to Texas with my brothers. We'd bought a herd, driven it north, and sold it.

I leaned forward, spoke to Grafton and Halifax. "If we push it," I said, "we'll be home in a couple of hours."

We went fast on the empty road, and my excitement turned to uneasy. Nobody was in the fields we passed, and the houses looked deserted. Farmers should've been tending to crops, and smoke should've been curling dark from chimneys. Women and children should've been feeding stock in the yards. Farm after farm was still as a painting, as if everyone had slept through morning, or flocked to an urgent call.

I told myself maybe a neighbor had needed assistance. Maybe there was a new barn to raise, a wedding, or a christening. It was a good day for celebration. The sky arched like a blue cathedral, a solitary hawk against it, the enormous eye of a warm and healing sun.

In a little while the world of my growing up was on us, and it was all as I remembered. Every tree and field and well-kept fence, every house and barn, every stone by the road called out to me in welcome.

We came to the curve where the road began to rise, and when we reached the top we'd be there. Joy spread in my chest. It seemed I'd been gone for years. Even though I didn't plan to stay, it was a fine thing to have a home to come to. We kicked those horses to the top of the hill and stared at what was below us.

"Jesus," Grafton said.

I looked at Halifax. A muscle jumped in his jaw, and his eyes were batting. Grafton's mouth was open. It looked like the hole in a birdhouse.

I turned back to the destruction, and a deep, cold fear grew inside me. The house was reduced to its gray stone foundation. A doorframe stood like a sentry protecting what was already gone. The barn was burned so completely the outline of its shape left markings on the ground that looked like a child's first drawing. Chickens wandered stupidly through a wasteland of dead pigs and cows. The fields nearest the house were burned to a blue-black stubble. The field beyond them had not been disturbed. The corn was tall and full. The tops swayed in the breeze.

I looked at what had been my home. The outhouse had survived.

Me and my brothers looked at one another, but didn't speak. I was thinking of my mother and Caesar, afraid to say their names, as if to do so would make certain that the worst had happened. I tried to control the fear and it turned to rage. I closed my mouth. If it stayed open, I'd cry out from loss and the absence of those who'd done this. I wanted to hurt them. I wanted to do it slowly, with unforgiving care.

I spurred my horse, hard and vicious, and we rode down the sunlit hill.

We walked through the ruin. My feet struck pieces of our lives. Pots and pans, burned photographs, dishes, bits of cloth, arms of furniture I'd dusted as a kid. In my mouth the taste of burned things promised to stay forever.

None of us spoke, none of us said we were looking for Caesar and our mother. Every time I moved something I expected to come upon their bodies, faces up, mouths open in disbelief.

We didn't find them. I didn't know whether to hope for the best, but I did anyway, because I think that's what men do in times of deepest trouble. I told myself that Caesar was resourceful. He'd spirited my mother away. Before long, when he understood the danger was past, he'd return. Even now he might be making his way toward us, and if I waited I'd see them coming through the corn, waving, calling my name. Or maybe they'd gone to Amelia's.

I looked toward the fields and saw the cornstalks moving in rhythms of grief, and the sun was like a blessing, and my rage was steady rising. I took the risk of looking at my brothers. Despite the abundant sunshine, their faces were overcast and pinched, as if they searched through the landscape of a frozen winter day.

I closed my eyes. We'd ride to Amelia's. Perhaps my mother and Caesar were safe at their spread.

When I said this to my brothers, they didn't answer, just turned and headed for their horses. We mounted, and the horses turned in a circle, and Halifax cried out, "Bastards," and I took a last look over my shoulder.

It was a little more than three miles to Amelia's, and on

the way I saw what I'd missed in my excitement at nearing home. The road was recently traveled, the signs of horses and wagons clear and unmistakable. The neighbors had gone this way. Now I doubted that they gathered for celebration, and I kicked my horse again, wanting to get to Amelia's to find out, wanting not to know, wanting to turn time back so none of this had happened.

When we arrived, the funeral services were over. They'd buried Caesar and my mother side by side on the top of a hill that rolled down from the barn. The soil was dark and moist and banked with rocks, and the flowers were white and purple. The graves faced east toward a fallow field and beyond it the spruce were rising.

Me and my brothers knelt alone, and the neighbors kept a respectful distance. Then Grafton and Halifax slumped to the side of the house where tables were stacked with food. Amelia came to stand beside me at the graves. She touched my shoulder, and I rose. She took my arm and looked at me with love and sadness, and we walked toward the gathered people. They were good folks, I knew them all, and they expressed their sympathy.

I told Amelia's parents how much I appreciated that they'd buried my people right. They nodded and said I was welcome. Then they didn't know what to say. The mother was wringing her hands, and her husband didn't meet my eyes. I couldn't help them. I didn't know what to say, either.

''Are you hungry?'' Amelia asked.

I wasn't. I heard a shout to my left and I turned to see children chasing across the yard. Someone hollered at them, and they stopped their play, slunk back to their families' sides.

I saw a tall man with a day-old beard and a silver star

on his chest. When I asked, Amelia said he was the sheriff come from Highland, the nearest town. I nodded and closed my eyes for a moment. When I opened them, Amelia was looking at me, worried, waiting for me to speak. But I didn't have anything to say. I was having trouble feeling. I knew I should be feeling something, but there wasn't anything there.

"Do you want to go inside?"

"No," I said.

"Come," she said. "Walk with me."

She put my arm in hers, led me toward a corner of the yard where flowers rioted in the sun. A bench was built next to the garden, and we sat. I looked across the way and saw the schoolhouse. The first time I kissed Amelia was behind that schoolhouse. I think I was fourteen.

Things were racing in my head, and I tried to get them to still, so I could choose one to consider. Here I was, finally, next to the woman I'd planned to marry. I'd come back home, successful. My farm was burned, my mama and Caesar dead. Now a voice began to call in me. I listened, but all it said was "Why?"

I thought how death had looked me up all through my journey and was waiting for me when I returned. I thought of all the deaths I'd had a part in, and I wondered if this was my due.

I asked Amelia how much she knew of what had happened. She took my hand in hers, and told me. White men had raided the farm the afternoon before. They'd passed her house just after noon. The lead rider on the biggest horse she'd ever seen.

It wasn't the first time marauding men had come through to cause some mischief, to kill a cow or two, to set fire to a haystack. Never anything serious, just small and mean. Some said it was men still fighting the Civil War, upset with the way it had ended, about having to compete on even terms with coloreds for jobs, furious that colored folks could vote, own property. She didn't know why they'd left her place alone, or why they'd chosen my mama's. She didn't even have any reason to suspect they were up to no good, except that when they passed, something about them set her to worry. She hitched a horse to a wagon and headed to my mama's farm. When she got there, she kept her distance, hiding in the trees that grew by the side of the road. She saw the men in front of the house, talking to Caesar. Caesar had a rifle in his hand. My mama was in the doorway. Amelia didn't know what was said, but suddenly a shot rang out and Caesar fell. Then the men just seemed to go crazy. Some of them went into the house, began to ransack it. Others headed for the barn. Soon they set fires. My mama began to run toward where Amelia was hiding. They shot my mama and she crumpled.

The funny thing, Amelia said, is that they didn't take much of anything, at least that she could see.

She waited until the men left. Then she rode back home to get her father, and the two of them came back. Her mother went to alert the neighbors and someone was sent to Highland to notify the sheriff.

Caesar was dead. My mother was dead. They loaded the bodies onto the wagon and brought them back to Amelia's. They stored the bodies in the icehouse for the night, and in the morning made them ready for the grave.

She released my hand, and it felt cool where she had held it. "I found out one thing they took," she said.

"What was that?"

"Caesar's medallion."

I nodded.

She paused and took a deep breath, and I saw tears in her eyes. She said that was it, nothing left to do but the funeral. If they'd known we were so near to home, they'd have waited. But they hadn't known.

She touched my shoulder, rubbed it hard, and I pulled her into my arms. Her head was against my chest, and I was thinking how long it had been since I'd held her, and how much I'd missed it. But now that she was in my arms, I wasn't comforted. I didn't long for her. It was rage, not love that called in me. I think Amelia felt it. She leaned back, looked into my eyes, and I let her look, and I saw something flicker in her face, uncertainty or fear.

Then she asked me a question folks had forever asked the grieving. "You all right?"

"No," I said. "I'm not."

My voice said her question was stupid. I couldn't look at her. I felt a sudden tiredness, like I'd been cut off from whatever had been keeping me going. I wanted to be with my brothers. Or alone.

"So how was the trip?" she said.

"Okay."

"Successful?"

I nodded. "More so than we'd planned."

"You'll tell me about it later."

I nodded and looked behind me, but I couldn't see my brothers. I looked out over the fallow field at the schoolhouse, the evergreens threatening to fly.

"Joshua?"

I didn't answer.

"God will help you through this."

I kept looking at the evergreens.

She went to her knees before me. "If you let Him, God will comfort."

"No," I said, "He won't."

She looked startled.

"Get up, Amelia," I said. "I want to go be with my brothers."

She got up. I could tell she wanted to say something, but she didn't know what. As we walked back to the house, she put her hand in mine. It felt funny.

The neighbors were eating. Some of them looked up at me and nodded, and some of them stopped talking. I asked had anyone seen my brothers, and five or six hands pointed.

"Stay here," I said to Amelia.

Grafton and Halifax were sitting beneath a tree behind Amelia's house, passing a bottle between them. I sat down, stuck my hand out, and Halifax handed the whiskey to me.

I said, "Those men we saw last night? It was them what done it."

Grafton asked, "The guy on the big horse?"

I nodded.

"Let's go," Halifax said.

I looked at him.

"I'm tired of people killing those I love," he said. "It's beginning to wear on me."

Grafton drank from the bottle.

"They killed my mama," Halifax said. "A woman never done nothing but try to help people. They killed Caesar."

His jaw was clenched. His eyes looked like a snake's. But he wasn't drunk. He was too mad to get drunk.

My own rage was settled, burning slow in a way that said it was permanent.

"They were headed northeast," I said. "If they ride steady, they'll have a day and a half, two days' lead on us."

Grafton said to me, "You considering going after them?"

"I am."

"Taking the law into our own hands?"

"I'm considering making sure the law gets their hands on them. If we don't point them out, how's the law ever going to know who done this?"

"Just kill the bastards," Halifax said.

"No," I said. "We'll bring them back."

Grafton snorted. "There was near a dozen men in that gang. How you gonna get that many men back here?"

I knew Grafton was making sense. I just didn't want to hear it. "We'll figure that out when we find them."

"Forget about bringing them back," Halifax said quietly. "We find and kill the bastards."

"We ain't killing nobody," I said. "If we don't agree on that, I ain't going."

Grafton stared at me, and said it again. "How you aim to get a dozen killers back here?"

I stared back at him. "We don't have to bring them back here. We have to find them. Then we go to the nearest sheriff and tell him where they are."

"And a sheriff's gonna believe us? Ain't gonna ask for proof? Three colored men walk into his jail and want him to arrest a bunch of white men?"

"I can't solve every problem before it happens."

"I'm not saying to solve every problem. Just this one."

"We can hire some men," I said. "Bounty hunters."

"And where we going to find them?" Grafton said.

"I don't know. But we will."

"I don't like it," Grafton said.

I said, "I don't like it, either. But I'm not going to let this go without trying to do something about it. Not while I can move and breathe."

Grafton still looked skeptical, but Halifax was nodding his head.

I said, "We need to get moving first thing in the morning."

*   *   *

Now that we had a plan, I was able to eat. By the time I'd
finished my plate, the neighbors were leaving. I stood at
the edge of the yard with my brothers, and we thanked them
one and all.

When they were gone the world felt empty. I wasn't
sleepy. I didn't want to talk. My brothers had gotten their
hands on a second bottle of whiskey, but I didn't feel like
drinking. So they headed off to the woods by themselves.

I sat with Amelia and her parents awhile, but it was like
sitting with the dead. I went outside and cared for all three
of our horses. When I'd finished that, I sat at one of the
tables in the yard and cleaned my pistol and rifle. I walked
three times around the house. I sat by the side of the fresh-
dug graves, thinking of all that happened.

Amelia came out of the house and said she'd fixed up
sleeping places in the barn. I said thank you, and she lin-
gered until she'd figured I wanted to be alone. When she
left, I went inside the barn. I stretched out and closed my
eyes and dreamed of cattle as far as the eye could see.

When I awoke, the sun was going down. I got up and
walked back to the house. My brothers were eating at the
kitchen table. I told them we ought to bed down right after
they ate, so we could leave before dawn. I told them I
planned to leave the money with Amelia. She'd put it in
the bank for us. We figured out how much money we
needed to take with us.

I ate a little something myself. Before I went to bed, I
walked outside with Amelia. For a while we sat on the
porch in silence; then she began to hum. I recognized the
song from church. I could see her face in the lamplight that
came from inside the house.

Then she stopped humming, and we both watched the

fireflies in the dark. "One day you'll tell me about the cattle drive," she said.

I said I would.

"Did you remember to pray?"

"Sometimes."

The question annoyed me, and maybe she sensed it, because she moved closer, took my arm, leaned her head on my shoulder.

"Joshua, I'm so sorry about your mother and Caesar."

I put my arm around her. "I know," I said.

"I'll help you heal," she promised. "I think we should get married right now, sell the farm, and leave here. Go to Montana like we said."

It came out in a rush, like a breath she'd been holding. I didn't answer.

"Joshua?"

"Yes?"

"I know this is a hard time for you, but you . . . something doesn't feel right. I mean . . . it's . . . do you still love me?"

I didn't know what I felt, but I said that I did.

"Then let's get married and leave here."

"I can't. Not yet."

"Why?"

"Two reasons. One is I owe some money to a man in Mexico."

"I don't understand."

"I bought some cattle from him on credit. He sent along two of his men who were going to bring the money back, but they got killed."

"How'd they get killed?"

"It's a long story."

"Okay. You'll tell me one day?"

I didn't think I would, but I nodded.

"And what's the second reason?"

"I'm going after those men who killed my mama and Caesar."

"Joshua. There's the law for that."

"That's why I'm going after them. To make sure the law does what it's supposed to."

"I don't like it," she said. "Anything can happen. I don't want to lose you."

"You won't lose me."

"We've waited so long to start our life together."

"We'll just have to wait a little longer."

"Joshua, what's happened to you? You don't sound the same."

I took a deep breath and looked out into the darkness between us and the schoolhouse. I couldn't see a thing.

"I don't know, Amelia. Maybe I'm not. Maybe I just need some time to sort out all that's happened. But in the meantime, I know what I have to do. And that's go after those men and make sure they face justice."

I could hear the echo of her question asking what had happened to me. If I knew the answer I'd have told us both.

I said, "I need you to do me a favor."

"What's that?"

"You and your daddy take the money into town and put it in the bank for us."

She said she would. "When will you leave?"

"In the morning."

"I'll make breakfast before you go, and fix some food to take with you."

"We're leaving before dawn."

"Wake me."

"How am I going to do that without disturbing your parents?"

"Tap on my window. I don't think I'll sleep much anyway. Please don't go without saying good-bye.''

I started to say that I could say good-bye now, but I didn't.

"How long do you think you'll be gone?"

"As long as it takes."

"I won't know where you are. I can't write to you."

"I can write to you."

"And you'll come back to Missouri before you go to Mexico?"

I said I would.

"We can get married then, and I can go with you to Mexico. We won't have to be apart for so long."

I thought about it. Maybe it wasn't such a bad idea after all. Traveling with a woman might afford me some protection.

"We'll see," I said. "We'll talk about it when I get back."

She put her arms around me, and moved in such a way that she was almost on my lap, and it was as if I was discovering for the first time how tall she was. She raised her mouth to mine, and we kissed. She made a sound in her throat that sounded like half-crying, half-laughing, and when our mouths parted we both were breathing deep. She looked up at me, love and trust in her eyes, and I bent to kiss her again. This time I held tighter, and her breasts were against my chest. I felt what was happening between my thighs. I put my hand on her leg, and began to pull her dress up, but she caught my hand with her own.

"No," she said. "Not now."

I fought my frustration, eased my grip around her waist. Then I told her I had to get some sleep. She sighed and said okay, and we stood, and she came into my arms again, all of her body against me, and we kissed, and I broke away, and headed for the barn.

Since I'd slept that afternoon, I wasn't sleepy at all. I lay considering the state Amelia had left me in.

I turned on my side, staring across the barn floor, thinking of my mama and Caesar. I sat up, and reached for the lantern. I felt for my saddlebag, and found paper and something to write with. I went outside and fired the lantern, and wrote a note to Amelia. I'd see her when I got back.

CHAPTER EIGHTEEN

We headed out just before dawn, when the world is still and dark and reeks of loneliness. I had a twinge of remorse when I went toward Amelia's window to stick my note beneath the windowsill. I tried not to look at the house. Half of me felt she'd be there, standing at the window, silent, disapproving. I looked anyway, and my heart jumped at a motion. But it was nothing, just my guilty imagination and the breeze that moved a tree branch.

I took a breath and looked out over the darkened fields where a thin, gray mist rose two feet off the ground. I said good morning to my brothers. I kept my voice low, but it still sounded like shouting in the stillness. We turned our horses toward the road.

Then I stopped. My brothers looked at me.

"Amelia fixed food for us to take," I explained.

If they'd accused me of not being right in the head, I'd have had to admit it. But they didn't.

I headed back to the house, went up the porch steps. In the front room the furniture squatted like creatures from a child's bad dream. The floor creaked a complaint about my weight. I felt outside of myself, watching myself. I knew what I was feeling didn't make any sense, but I'd latched on to the notion that while it was all right to leave without saying good-bye to Amelia, I couldn't go without the food. She'd understand my not waking her, but she wouldn't forgive my not taking what she'd prepared for me to eat.

The food was on the table, bundled in a cloth. I fixed its position in my mind's eye, then looked quickly back at the doorway. I felt like a thief. I picked up the food and went outside, divided it with my brothers. There was chicken and biscuits and baked yams, and it smelled good in the morning. Maybe it was the smell that made me think of my mama and Caesar, the two of them in brand-new graves on the slope behind the barn. I'd never see them again in this life. And yet it seemed I was leaving them at the time they needed me most, and that I was to blame for what had happened. All of it was mixed up, grief and guilt in the sullen pre-dawn light.

We pushed the food into our saddlebags, and I took a deep breath, and we rode, no sound but the clop of horses' hooves on the road and the rustle of unseen living things in the brush and trees that lined it. The mist above the land was rising, disappearing before it reached the height of my horse's belly, as if mist time on earth was carefully allotted and had to end before the sun arrived.

We came to what was left of the farm, the doorframe standing like an altar in the gloom. The loss of my loved ones rose in me, and I grit my teeth and told myself to control it.

We moved past our devastated home at a pace that was slow and steady. We rode to the top of the hill, and then we stopped and looked below us into the retreating dark. I felt something between me and the world, something that made it hard to see things as they were, as if the waning dark had thickness. I wished the rage would come back. Rage would keep me going, blunt my grief.

I said to my brothers, "Let's go."

As we rode, the sky began to brighten, and the world awakened to a half-dozen roosters. I could see activity in the farmhouses we passed, smoke coming from a chimney, in a window a lantern like a yellow eye, and now I could make out the cornstalks in the fields, and birds were everywhere singing.

We rode, and the sun came up, and the fields seemed to rise to meet it. The farmers went in and out of their barns, and all of them waved to us, and I thought their movements were sad.

We rode until the sun was high, and then we stopped to eat and to water the horses. Halifax opened his food. He took out a piece of folded paper from beneath a chicken leg. He opened the paper, read it.

"For you," he said.

The note said: "Joshua, I love you. Be careful. Come back to me."

I folded it and put it in my pocket. Amelia had known I wouldn't say good-bye. Grafton asked me what I was shaking my head for, and I didn't tell him how everything was mixed up inside me. I fell back on the tried and true. "Women," I said, and he grunted as if that word held all the world's mysteries. But the silence that Halifax sat in seemed to deepen, and when I glanced at him, he was staring at his feet, his profile carved from stone that was deep and brown and ancient. I was reminded that in addition to my mama and Caesar, Halifax was grieving for Rachel. I wanted to say something to him about it, but I didn't know what. He must have felt me looking at him, because he turned, and blinked, and held my gaze for a moment before he looked away.

"How you doing?" I asked.

"Fine," he said. "How you doing?"

I heard the mocking in his voice, and I realized I'd done it too, asked that stupid question of someone who was grieving.

"Ready to ride?"

He nodded. "Let's go."

"I beg your pardon," I said.

His eyebrows arched. "For what?"

"For asking a damn-fool question."

He smiled a thin, sad smile. "Apology accepted."

We rode through the afternoon, and our way was empty except for a traveler or two heading south, a farmer gone to town for supplies, a poor white family with all its earthly belongings in a wagon that rolled unbalanced for needing a new back wheel. The father, a blue bandanna around his neck, was driving, eyes hidden by a hat brim pulled so low it nearly touched his nose. His wife sat next to him, hands folded, face sharper than an ax. I wondered where they'd come from, why they'd pulled up stakes. I asked myself was it a better life they headed to, and what was their destination.

And then we got lucky. We came across a group who'd heard that a gang had burned down a farm north of Springfield. One of the men was riding a big gray horse.

Springfield was to the west of us. We were headed east. We thanked them and turned in the right direction.

A couple of hours later, other roads began to feed into the one we traveled, and now there were people everywhere, walking in twos or threes, alone, on horseback, and in wagons. It felt like the whole country had gotten up this morning and decided to take off in the direction of Springfield on their way to parts unknown.

The day was winding down, and I began to think of the task before us. I wondered if I'd made a foolish choice in deciding to follow a gang of killers to only God-knew-where. These were men, not cattle who could be herded despite their wishes. I pushed away the feeling, thought about my mama and Caesar. I was trying to make the rage come back, but all I felt was grief, and dumb for what I was doing.

Just before evening we caught up to a black family in a spanking-new Conestoga. The kids had faces as bright as new pennies. The boys had been taught to walk with their backs straight and to look you in the eye, and the girls had their hair oiled and plaited. The grandparents smiled at us out of faces lined with wisdom. They were from Tennessee, on their way to Nebraska to claim what the government had promised: forty acres and a mule. They were joining family there. They said things were bad in Tennessee; slavery might be over, but for black folks times were still as hard as week-old corn bread.

Instead of kicking our horses and trying to get a few more miles in before the sun set, we rode with them. When dark began to fall, we camped off the side of the road in a clearing ringed by oak trees. The women prepared food for us. The father sang and played a guitar while we sat around a fire.

When the father asked me where we were on our way to, I told him we were looking for some bad men who'd done some things they had to pay for. He grinned and said if I was looking for bad men in this country, I wouldn't have far to go.

One of the children cried out in the wagon, as if frightened by a dream. I heard a woman speak soothingly to it, and I remembered my mother being there when I'd awakened scared of what lurked in the dark.

We sat until the fire burned down, and then the father said he was turning in, and we said we'd do the same.

We slept, we rose in the morning, and the sun came up in a ball of brand-new gold. We ate and said good-bye to the family, and hoped to meet again. Heading north/northwest, we bypassed Springfield, found the quiet of open country. The sky was wearing one of those blues that seemed painted, and the sun was warm on my shoulders.

We stopped at the first farmhouse we came to. There was a young woman in the yard, barefoot, heavy with child, brown hair down to her waist. She was hanging laundry on a line, the clothes so white I blinked. She was uneasy in our presence, and I tried to speak and move in ways that wouldn't frighten her. I told her who we were looking for. She remembered the men and the huge horse; she'd been outside two days before when they went by. The man on the big horse had tipped his hat to her. She said they were headed due west.

I thanked her and we got back on the road. We came to the farm the gang had destroyed. The people were collected in small bunches. The few livestock were slaughtered, some with their throats cut. These lay on their sides and the flies feasted on the dried pools of their blood. The gang had taken food and what money was in the house. They'd burned down the house and the barn. They'd left the fields, the garden. They hadn't killed anyone.

We resumed our journey, rode all day. We came to a town that had a hotel, and we put up there for the night. The hotel clerk said the gang had come through a couple of days ago, in the middle of the afternoon, but had only stopped to eat and drink. They seemed in a hurry, and didn't make a bother.

We ate downstairs near the bar, a room with a broken

mirror and a filthy floor. Some of the whores were black and some were white. Two of them smiled at me, but I ignored them. I had that feeling again, like I was standing behind a wall. I could see over the wall to the world beyond it. I could smell the world and touch it, but the world couldn't touch me.

I studied the men in the room. They looked tired and defeated. They clung to whiskey bottles as if what was inside held magic or the promise of lasting peace. I wondered what made men do what they did, what drove them to destroy, what made them kill the innocent? How many of these men had taken a life, how many would willingly do it again?

One of the men at the table nearest me fell face-forward on the table. Someone picked his head up by the hair, and he puked all over his chest.

That night I slept without dreaming. I awoke rested, my mind was clear. I looked in the room's dirty mirror. I needed a shave. All during the cattle drive, I'd shaved at least every other day. I always liked a clean-shaven look. But now I decided not to. The stubble made me look older, and serious.

We went downstairs and ate breakfast, and me and my brothers barely said a word, and the silence was right and welcome. We went outside and mounted up and headed away from the sun. The men we followed had left the road and cut across country, and although we couldn't travel as fast, it was easier now to track them. The big horse had feet suitable to his size, and left unmistakable footprints.

We rode and the land grew hilly and parched, and the farms were few and far between. At noon the next day we came across the remains of a camp the gang had made in a hollow left by hills. We figured we were still a day and a half behind them. Grafton squatted at what had once been a fire, poked through it with a stick.

"Where you think they headed?" he asked.

I said I didn't know. "Maybe Oklahoma. Or Kansas. I don't think Arkansas. They'd have turned south by now."

Grafton grunted. "Ain't nothing in Oklahoma."

"Maybe," I said, "maybe not."

All of a sudden the temperature dropped, and I looked off to the west where dark clouds gathered like bad luck at the horizon.

"Getting ready to storm."

"Looks pretty bad," Grafton said.

We got back on our horses and rode to the top of a hill so we could look for shelter. We saw a farmhouse in the distance, maybe an hour away. The sky was getting darker. It was weird to watch night fall in the middle of the afternoon. We came to the spread, and the farmer, who hadn't seen hair nor hide of anyone in more than a week, said we could ride out the storm in his barn.

It rained the rest of that day and all night. The wind blew like it had something personal against us. I thought the walls would cave in, or the roof fly off. The rain drummed a martial beat. The pigs and cows were shifting and moaning, and I had Halifax stand by our horses to keep them settled.

Then the wind shifted, changed pitch, began to scream like someone wounded, and when I looked through the crack in the barn door, I couldn't see a thing. I rubbed a hand across my face and surprised myself at the stubble. I was cold and wet and miserable, wondering what the hell I was doing here.

Halifax walked over to me, and I moved aside so he could look outside for himself.

"I hate these kind of storms," he said. "Make me feel like the world is closing in."

I said I knew what he meant.

"Dark and cold," he said. "And trapped."

"We'll get through this," I said. "You'll get through it."

For a while I thought he wasn't going to answer, and then he said, "I guess so. But what'll I be when I do?"

"You'll be Halifax. You'll know a little bit more about life. You'll know it isn't always fair."

"Rachel," he said, as if we'd been talking about her all along, "was the best thing ever happened to me."

I nodded, even though his back was turned to me. I was remembering that she'd said the same thing about Halifax.

"What a stupid way to die," he said. "And now it feels like something's dead in me. And I don't have the time to figure out what, 'cause on top of that comes my mama and Caesar."

"You'll figure it out," I said. "There'll be time for that."

"Rachel told me she talked to you. She really appreciated the way you listened. She liked you."

A hole opened up in my stomach. "I liked her."

"I'm so full of mad, Josh. And empty. Don't know what I'm going to do. We're trailing these men, and we'll find them, and do what we have to do, and then what? What'll I do after that? What's worthwhile doing?"

"We can go home. Rebuild the farm."

"I thought about that. I don't want to. I don't want to be there, remembering all that's happened."

"I've got to head for Mexico to give Romero his money back. I'd ask you to come with me, but it ain't safe."

"I know," he said, and shook his head. "I'm a wanted

man in Texas. Wanted for murdering two men I shot in self-defense.''

''We'll figure something out,'' I said.

It sounded weak and insincere, and it was, because I didn't have any faith right then that we'd figure anything out. I just knew we'd survive, changed perhaps, but we'd go on living. The world was a hard place. Sometimes it gave in a little and tricked you into thinking you could have your way if you just worked hard and believed. Then life turned its back on you, left you standing with your jaw down to your chest, the latest edition of a newly minted fool.

Toward morning the storm stopped, and all of us slept a little, and this time I dreamed, and in the dream it was night, and I was hunted for killing a man. I didn't know the man's name or why I killed him. I didn't remember the killing. I was running away from a city of lights into darkness, and I looked to see who was behind me. There was no one there. Just before I started falling, it came to me: the man I had killed was me. The understanding was quiet and rueful, like remembering where you set down the hat you'd spent the last ten minutes in search of.

I woke up shaking my head at the way dreams could make no sense at all. I went to the barn door, and the sun was bright, and the world wore shining puddles. The farmer invited us for breakfast into a house that was quieter than death and filled with flowers. Flowers were in vases and jars, in the parlor, the kitchen, lighting up the house with a sweet smell that leaned toward sickly. The farmer's wife was a skinny, poorly looking woman. I searched for something in her that hinted of a love for color and growing things, but I didn't see it. The farmer told us that the land here had once been rich, but now it wasn't fit for much.

He was thinking about pulling up stakes and heading out, maybe to Nebraska. I learned he was the one who'd grown the flowers in a bed out behind the barn that he kept rich with manure. It was him who'd placed the flowers all around the house.

We ate and thanked them and set off again, and we rode for an hour and had to admit we'd lost the trail. The storm had swallowed it. I sat there, slumped, looking in all directions. The hills we'd passed through a half a day before were well behind us, and the land stretched like a Texas plain. I could see a wagon that had been abandoned, its rear wheels missing, its frame bleached from the sun. We got off our horses, squatted.

I said, "Which way, now?"

"Who are they?" Grafton said.

"Meaning?"

"Who are they? What are they up to? Where do they come from and do they have a destination? And is there a purpose?"

"Why do they have to have a purpose?"

"Because people usually do."

"I don't know," I said. "Folks do things sometimes and think up a reason later."

"We got to figure they got some kind of plan. If not, chances are we'll never find them. They could do anything, go anywhere at anytime. Like chasing tumbleweed."

Halifax was looking at Grafton with this intense expression on his face. He turned to me. "Grafton's got a point," he said. "Why would a dozen men ride together? Where they going? They burn our farm for a reason? Because we're colored?"

I said, "The farm outside of Springfield wasn't colored. Besides, I don't care why they done it. I just want to find them."

I didn't understand until later why I was annoyed. It was because I'd wanted to keep my questions secret, I didn't want my doubts to sap our will. Somehow I had the feeling that if the questions were spoken, we'd pack up and head home. Maybe my brothers understood this, because neither remarked at the edge in my voice.

"You mentioned tumbleweed," said Halifax. "They could be drifters."

"They could be anything," Grafton said, "but chances are they're up to something. If we can figure that out, we can guess their next move."

"Suppose they're still fighting the war," I said. "Roaming the country, burning colored farms. Suppose the farm outside Springfield was an exception, or they thought the hired hands were the owners."

"Doesn't add up," Grafton said. "If that's their purpose, then they'd want to go into Nebraska. That's where you've got the biggest passel of coloreds homesteading. And they'd have turned north long ago if they were headed for Nebraska."

I looked at Grafton, but he wasn't looking at me.

"But still," he said, "that's a lot of hate and energy. I can't imagine nobody putting in all that energy just to bother colored folks. They could have stayed in the south and done that. People can only do things for hate for a little while, then they start looking for gain."

Halifax was nodding his head.

"Maybe they're bank robbers," I said. I was struggling with the feeling of being younger than my brothers.

Halifax said in a quiet voice, "Why'd they bypass Springfield?"

"Because that bank's too hard to rob," I said. "Remember back in '68 when that gang out of Topeka tried to?"

The attempt had been a disaster. All seven gang members had died.

Halifax said, "If I was a bank robber and looking for some place to hit, I'd go to Sedalia. All that money changing hands on an almost-daily basis. Drunk, just-paid cowboys, and a handful of lawmen. That's where I'd go."

"Sedalia's a week's ride from here. North and east. Their trail's been leading west."

Neither answered me. Halifax was drawing with a stick in the ground. Grafton was staring off into the distance.

I said, "You still all right with this? You want to put a limit? Call it off if we can't find them before some time we agree on?"

Grafton looked at me the way he did in Abilene, like he was just discovering me. Halifax cursed, and said, "Hell, no, we'll follow them bastards to the ends of the earth. We'll find them."

Something sank in me, but I didn't let it show. "Then, let's go," I said. "We keep heading west, to Kansas, until we pick up their trail. Somebody will have seen them."

I put some energy in my voice, but I felt like a man with a hammer trying to break up a mountain of rock.

CHAPTER NINETEEN

So we headed for Kansas, on faith, or stupid stubbornness. We rode across dry and yellow land, went hard the day, camped at night, got an early start in the morning.

Two days later, the country turned like a page in a book of landscapes, became wooded with pine and birch and oak, crossed with clear streams, grassy fields that danced with goldenrod. I was beginning to feel on the doorstep of some kind of sickness, weak and hot with fever. I'd look up at the sky, and the blue would swirl and threaten to fall, or I'd have to stare at a tree until it became familiar. The steady pounding of hoofbeats collected in my stomach. I began to imagine snakes thick as my arms, coiled and ready to strike in the path before me, and my heart would start to race. A couple of times Grafton asked was I all right, and I said I was, but I wasn't.

At night, I'd have these dreams in which a nameless danger stalked me with a single-minded patience. I was unarmed and exhausted and although a safe place waited just around a turn, I was too weak to get there. I'd wake to a pitch-black dark, trying to recall the danger. All I could remember were bits and frightening pieces: Steele's scalped head, Rachel's face as it exploded, bad men's mangled bodies in a shallow grave.

In the morning, I'd be worn out, as if I'd worked through the night. I'd saddle up, force my body to horseback. I needed to have a goal, and so I told myself that I had to make it to Kansas. I didn't want to go to Kansas. I wanted to stay where I was, to sleep without dreaming. I'd grit my teeth and will my body to go on. I'd rub a hand across my face and my beard was full and thick.

On the second day we went through two thriving towns, four hours apart, outside of which were neat, abundant farms. In both towns we stopped and asked, but nobody had seen the men we searched for. We bought food supplies and took up our journey of faith. I kept the thought before me, it was my driving promise: I had to make it to Kansas.

Past the second town and its farms, my fever was high, and everything looked the same, hills and clouds, hawk and bounding rabbit. To counteract the sameness I dreamed: a ranch in Montana, peace, a clean, well-lighted place. Sometimes I made up the dreams, sometimes the fever did. Once, after we'd crossed a ridge that plunged to a rocky bottom, I imagined I had the gang in my sights and had begun a deliberate firing. Blood was everywhere, and their cries made me think of slaughtered pigs. Someone was saying, "Look what you done. Look what you done," and I looked and all I felt was nothing.

I came out of the dream, and my mouth was dry, and I asked myself hard questions. Why would I, who turned away from killing, imagine such a thing? It must have been the fever. I reached for my canteen, drank long and deep, and made my way toward Kansas.

*　　*　　*

The third day we rode for most of the day without a farm or a town in sight, and I was beginning to feel the journey in my rear end and in my shoulder blades. The backs of my thighs were knots, but I think the fever had gone down a little, because I was thinking more clearly. I didn't want to face it, but I'd made a bad decision. I'd acted on impulse. Those men were killers, and we weren't. If we found them, we could end up dead. If we didn't, we'd have spent a lot of time and effort and come up empty.

We weren't killers. The words sang in my head, mocking me, and I wiped my sweating brow. There was a trail of bodies behind us, at least one caused by my very own hand. What made me different from the men we were after? The fact that I preferred not to kill?

The sky tilted, and I shut my eyes until the dizziness went away, and I was feeling hot again. Grafton was riding next to me, and asked if I was all right. I don't know why I didn't tell him how poorly I was feeling, but I didn't.

I was thinking of those bounty hunters in Abilene, and how I'd shot to kill. I could have fired to wound. I'd spent my whole life practicing to do that, but I hadn't. I thought of the vision I'd had of wiping out the gang. It was the daydream of a killer.

Still, I didn't have to add to the wrongdoing by ending up in a place where I'd have to kill again. I wondered how my brothers would react if I called this journey off. "We're heading back," I'd say. "This whole thing was a bad idea."

I imagined both turning away in disgust, thinking me a coward, a man who didn't finish what he'd started, a man who left the murder of his family unavenged. The thought hung above me like a knife, and I knew if it fell it would leave a wound that would take a long time healing.

I'd give it at least to Kansas. If we hadn't found those

men by then, I'd turn back. Even if my brothers didn't
agree with me, I was out of it after that. They could do
what they wanted, think as they pleased. I'd head back to
the farm, get the money from Amelia, turn south to Mexico
to pay Romero back. Maybe I'd take Amelia with me.

Thinking that made me feel like a traitor to my blood. I
couldn't win. If I stayed, I could end up dead, or doing
more killing. If I left, I'd be alive, but I'd be a loser.

My sickness was getting worse. My joints were sore. The
fever was high again, and I was hot one minute and cold
the next. The world still turned in sudden ways at times
when I least expected, but at least the snakes were gone.

Just before evening of that third day, we came to the top
of a hill and stared at what was below us. Who, I wondered,
had decided to build a town out here? There was nothing
around it but rich land spiked with timber, and green flowing hills, out of which, to our right, flowed a sparkling
silver stream. It was land that could easily have been
cleared for farming, but for whatever reason, nobody had
done it. And in the absence of farms, what could support
a town out here?

"Ain't this a surprise?" Halifax said.

I allowed that it was. "But we can get a decent meal,"
I said. "And a drink. And maybe sleep in a bed." I was
thinking that maybe that was all I needed to feel better.

"You getting soft in your old age," Grafton said, but I
could tell he was looking forward to it, too.

Halifax asked, "How far are we from the Kansas border?"

I thought about it. "Half a day. Maybe more."

He grunted.

We rode down the hill and found the road that just started
out of nothing, and we went past the remains of small

shacks, a half dozen in number, maybe a hundred yards apart. They'd been built in a hurry, and left just as quick. I saw pots and pans scattered on the ground, some in usable shape, some bent and battered. I saw the tattered remains of blankets worn out by weather, a boot, small piles of clothing, a perfectly good ax with its rusty head sunk in a tree. A clothesline sagged between two saplings.

"What you think those shacks were for?" Halifax asked.

I shook my head and the dizziness started again. I waited until it passed before saying I didn't know.

"Whoever was here sure left in a rush," Grafton said.

We rode into town in the half light of approaching evening. There weren't a lot of people on the streets, and the stores were closed. The bank, the post office and the jail were halfheartedly boarded up.

I saw some colored people on the street. They seemed to move carefully, and looked at us with surprise. They struck me as old, not so much in age, but as if they were from another time. We passed four white men, each one alone, who walked as if sick, or wounded. A faint smell hung above the town. The smell was troubled like the quiet, indescribable, like the light.

We left our horses at the stable. There were maybe a dozen animals there already, some stock-still, some shifting. They looked like abandoned children in stalls that were sweet with fresh straw. There was a black mutt who was blind in one eye. He raised his head and yawned at us before he went back to sleep. The blacksmith wore a porky hat, and looked like he came from Asia. His leather apron had a rip near one knee, and when he talked he'd pause to spit through the gap in his two front teeth.

We walked toward the hotel. I looked up and the hills wore a cloak of purple. Beyond them the sky was black. I smelled that funny smell again. I still couldn't say what it was.

The hotel was open, but it wasn't exactly thriving. At the tables throughout the room sat ten men, four in a game of cards that was beginning to build some interest. The whores were pretending to be indifferent, lounging like bait in traps set for the unsuspecting. There were five of them. Two were colored, one in a once-white dress below eyes that were dull and cowlike, another so fat you couldn't see her neck. The fat one had a scar on her forehead. Against the chocolate brown of her skin, it shone like a crescent moon.

The light in the room was funny, bright enough to see by, but undefined and yellow. It made me squint, and my stomach tilted. I ordered a drink, and the feeling settled in my gut when I took it.

The one thing I was sure of was wanting to eat, and the drink put an edge on my hunger. I ordered beef and potatoes, and had another whiskey while I waited for it to arrive.

The beef was cooked to black. It covered half the plate, and blood seeped from its bottom. I cut into it. The inside was red and raw, and as I stared, it seemed to throb in protest of its fate.

I gagged and understood my sickness. It had nothing to do with my body and all to do with my soul. I'd killed that bounty hunter back in Abilene. I was wanted by the law in Texas, and my mother and Caesar were slaughtered, and it was my fault. The punishment for what I'd done was in the deaths of innocents, Rachel and Romero's men included. My sickness was my crime.

My skin felt like it was heating up, and I thought if I moved, I'd be on fire. But if I didn't move, I'd never walk the earth in peace, never love or find the comfort that I craved, never see Montana. I had to move. If I'd been alone I'd have screamed and started running, because running seemed the only fit response, because the wind would cool my burning, and my screams make known what I'd done. I was less than worthless, a man who'd caused the deaths of his friends and family and broken his word to his self.

"You all right?" Grafton said. He was leaning toward me, and I blinked at his narrowed eyes. The men at the card table whooped and hollered, and Grafton's face seemed to float to me.

I smiled and shook my head. "I don't want to think," I said. "I want to forget."

"What?"

Halifax was looking at me like I'd gone loco. I laughed and ordered a bottle of whiskey from the woman with the pockmarked face and the bright red shoes who was winding between the tables.

"Let's drink," I said. "Let's drink to not remembering."

"Not remembering what?" Halifax said.

"Everything," I said. "Dead men and mothers rotting in the grave, women who love us, a world gone mad with killing."

"Josh," Halifax said, and I laughed and said it was all right, all I wanted was to forget and have a drink with my brothers.

I poured and drank and poured again. I drank until the room turned its dirty walls, and the whores were beautiful, and the men who sat with bottles were brave and good and true. I blinked and the whores were moving, and behind them, as if hypnotized, came the brave, true men into their baited traps. Somebody yelled again, and I saw a man in a mud-brown hat hold a card above his head. His hand trembled with the weight of triumph, and when it slapped the card against the table it moved slowly and spoke of grace.

I drank until a light pressed itself against the shapes of men and whores alike, and the light was pale blue and seemed to come from inside them. I was drawn to a man who threw back his head in laughter, the lines in his throat taut with blood that was visible and flowing. I knew this was the work of drink, so I wasn't afraid, but still, there was no forgetting, just a deepening of pain and the knowing I was lost.

Which is why, when the whore sidled over to me, all fluttering and eye-batting and skinny, I asked how much she would charge. When she gave me the price, I told Grafton to take care of my saddlebag and rifle. I gripped the arms of my chair, willing the room to stop turning, willing my body to rise.

"Wait a minute," Grafton said. He asked the whore to excuse us for a moment, and when she'd moved away, he looked at me. I was amazed by the depth of the lines that marked his furrowed brow.

"That's a white woman," he said.

"So?"

"We're in a place we don't know nothing about. And you know how folks are with this kind of thing."

I waved away Grafton's caution in a motion so sweeping my hand knocked my glass to the floor. "She's a whore. Ain't nobody here care who she goes upstairs with. I seen two white whores go with coloreds already. And the only two colored whores I seen gone off with whites."

Halifax said, "You sure you want to do this?"

"What about Amelia?" Grafton said.

I blinked to bring them both back into focus, and then I laughed. I laughed hard, tears came to my eyes, and I didn't know what I laughed at.

"What about her?" I asked.

Grafton shrugged. Halifax looked away. I waved to the

whore and she came to me, and I followed her up the stairs.
I was drunk. I'd only been under the influence this way a
few times in my life, the first as a kid when I discovered
a jug Caesar kept in the barn, a couple of times at weddings.
The world was spinning, and to keep from falling I held to
the whore's skinny arm. But I wasn't making excuses. I
knew what I was doing. And it wasn't easy. Half of me
was thinking I was simply trying to prove something to
myself, that when I got to the room, I'd say to the whore,
"You can go now. Thanks for helping me up the stairs."

I got past that by thinking of Amelia, her piety, how she
judged me with her eyes, the angle of her head, her shoulders. I thought of her touch, how she'd aroused me and
pushed my hand away. I thought about Rachel, and what I
felt for her, and how it had confused me, and now she was
dead. I opened the door and led the whore inside.

The bedspread was white with a stain in the middle that
looked like an Indian headdress. The pounding in my head
was the same as my heart's, like an echo, as if I stood inside
some chamber alive with muffled sound. I sat on the bed
and decided I needed a drink. I sent the whore back for the
bottle, took off my boots and began to consider my toes.
I'd gotten lost in the idea of toes, their shape and number,
the spaces between them, when she came back and handed
me the whiskey.

I drank and offered it to her. She refused, her eyes funny,
maybe with calculation, and I was glad I'd had the presence
of mind to leave my belongings with Grafton.

"What's your name?" I asked, and I heard my words
slur.

"Jennie," she said.

"Well, Jennie. I want you to help me forget. Can you
do that?"

She nodded, and I saw it wasn't calculation in her eyes. It was caution, a stray dog's suspicion of the offered hand. Something in me wanted to confess to her that this was my first time doing it for money, but I didn't. She was neither stray dog nor friend to tell my secrets to. She was a whore.

I lay back across the bed and told her to undress me, and as she did, the parts of my body that she exposed grew bumps in the coolish room. When she'd finished, she backed away, began her own disrobing. I watched in a blue haze while she bared breasts that sagged despite their small-ish size. She had a bit of a belly and hips leaner than a boy's. A horrid scar on her left thigh had been sewed by someone who wasn't very good at it.

I held out my hand and she stepped toward me, and I pulled her to the bed, dimly aware that I seemed harder than ever. I rolled her onto her back and climbed on top, and her legs opened, and for a moment we were face to face, our noses almost touching, and I found the sickening smell of her breath.

I turned my head and entered her with all the force I could gather, so hard she whimpered. I began to move in her tight and shallow dryness, each thrust bringing a sharp breath to her lips as though she were hurting, as I was from the absence of wet.

I pulled out of her. She watched as I spit onto my fingers, twice, and rubbed between her legs, and I felt the wiry hair grow softer, and the dry gave way to slippery. I got on top again.

It was easier now. I reached beneath her with both hands and held her butt, pulling her up to me, and it was deeper and worth the effort. I planned to stay there forever, to keep moving hard until I didn't remember.

"Yes," she said. "Do me. Yes."

I knew her passion was faked. I was no different than a thousand men before me. Yet I chose to believe that our connection was not about money, but affection and comfort, and in believing I managed to forget.

CHAPTER TWENTY

I awoke alone. Morning was a hammer at my head. My body felt as if I'd been beaten. My stomach was sour and my mouth a cave of cotton. The room smelled of coupled flesh and whiskey. I tried to swallow, but couldn't. I thought of my mother and Caesar and Amelia. If I'd had the strength, I'd have moaned.

But I didn't moan. I cursed. Cursed this violent country, cursed circumstance, cursed filthy hotel rooms and whores who sold a forgetting that was gone by the morning light.

Grafton banged on the door, asked how I was. I told him I'd live, but to please not to bang on the door. He said to come eat, I'd feel better. The thought of food made my eyes close.

"What time is it?" I asked.

" 'Bout a quarter to eleven."

I'd slept through morning. I couldn't remember the last time I'd done that. I told Grafton I'd be down in a while.

When he left, I just lay there, smelling my night of forgetting. I thought of water to bathe with, but I decided I wouldn't wash. I'd wear what I'd done, the smell and the grime of it. I'd wear it like a badge to show the world I understood it, I could deal on its terms and not back down. That gave me a sense of satisfaction so deep I grunted.

I swung out of bed and found that moving demanded having a plan. The body I'd known so well, that had served without my thinking, seemed reconstructed from the parts of strangers. My right leg needed to be introduced to my left. My shoulders didn't fit, and my head shouted at my stomach for having the gall to exist. I looked at my face in the mirror. The beard made me look like a desperado or a grim-faced hanging judge.

I took a deep breath and got myself together enough to dress, but I was as sick as I could be. I staggered downstairs and managed to sit at a table and shaded my eyes from the light. There were men sitting at three of the tables, staring at the floor or the bottles before them. I couldn't tell if they'd spent the night or were starting a brand-new day.

My brothers were looking at me with a mixture of worry and smiling.

"How you feel?" Halifax said.

"Don't ask," I said.

Grafton got up and ambled over to the bar. I looked around the room, at the men more still than statues. Grafton came back with a whiskey bottle and a glass. I watched as he poured two fingers of the foul-looking liquid. He pushed the glass toward me.

"Drink it. You'll feel better."

"You're crazy," I said.

"It's up to you," Grafton said. "You can keep feeling what you're feeling. Or you can drink this and feel better. Your choice."

I think he was trying not to smile. I looked at the nasty-looking whiskey. I looked at him. He was nodding, as if to say, "Go ahead."

I've got as much heart as the next man, and there have

been times in my life when I've showed it. But I think the bravest thing I'd done up till then was pick up that whiskey and drink it.

It left a fire in my throat and chest. It hit my stomach like a stone that had spent the night in an oven. I gasped and gagged, and my eyes began to water. The sour rose up in my nose. I moaned and put my head on the table, wheezing and wishing for death.

When I realized I felt better, I didn't trust it. But I was better. I wasn't my usual self, but it was clear I was going to live.

I sat up and said, "Whew."

My brothers were nodding and smiling like I'd just passed some test. Halifax said, "Now you got to eat something."

I shook my head. "Uh-uh."

"We been right so far?"

I stared at him. He went to the bar, and in a little while, somebody from the kitchen brought me a plate with two biscuits and bacon. It looked like slop for pigs.

"Go on," Grafton said. "Eat."

I took a bite of the bacon. It wasn't bad. I bit into the biscuit. My stomach fussed, but it didn't rebel. I ate everything on my plate. I wanted water.

"Hold off on drinking anything for a while," Halifax said.

I asked, "How come you guys know so much about this?"

" 'Cause we been there before."

I was human again, or at least half-human. I was sitting with my brothers, and I was glad they were with me. Somebody starting singing in an upstairs room, a wailing cowboy song, and I heard the shriek of a woman, and when I looked up, I saw her, half dressed, running along the landing. In hot pursuit was a fat man, as naked as the day he was born.

"I need some air," I said.

Grafton nodded. "Want some company?"

"No. Be back in a few."

I went outside. The sky was overcast, a sullen gray, and the air sagged with the threat of rain. I watched as a couple of cowboys, mean-looking and filthy, pushed an old man off the wooden sidewalk into the street. Then they took out their pistols, shot them into the sky for no reason whatever. Horses tied to hitching posts reared and neighed at the sound of the gunfire. Pigs and chickens walked the streets like they paid taxes. A thin black girl looked at me from the space between buildings. She was maybe ten, wearing a torn blue dress, barefoot, hair matted, face and legs coated with dirt, and she crouched like a cornered animal. I wondered where her folks were.

I passed a dead dog, shot in the side. His mouth was open and the blood had dried around the wound, and there were flies fighting for his flesh with a writhing mess of maggots.

The buildings looked like they'd been built overnight, with no thought to their lasting. When I turned in all directions, all I saw was that beautiful land stretching to the earth's four corners, making the town look as if someone with a bad temper had dropped it from the sky.

When I passed the jail, I was hit with a spell of dizziness, and I stopped and took a deep breath. When it eased, I continued walking, but I wasn't feeling too good. There was an old black man sitting on one of two chairs outside the general store, smoking a pipe, looking like he hadn't moved in the last century. I asked him if he'd mind me borrowing his chair, and he said no, and I sat down beside him.

Sitting made me realize how tired I was. For a while I

watched the confusion before me, wondering what this country was coming to, listening to the old man sucking on his pipe.

"What town am I in?" I asked.

"Elmerton."

He looked at me. For no reason I could determine, he smiled, and his gums were blue. He wore beat-up heavy boots and overalls that needed a wash.

"I came through two towns with not a colored in sight before I got here. Where'd these come from?"

He said from Tennessee, Kentucky, and Georgia. They'd come like a heap of other folks had, crazed with the promise of gold.

"Gold?"

"'Bout two years ago, found gold up there by the stream. Word got out, as word will," he said, "and 'fore you know it folks was coming in from everywhere. Built this town in about a minute. My boss man was part of it all."

"What happened?"

"You know how gold is. Here one minute, gone the next."

So that explained the shacks we'd seen riding in. "How long ago was that?"

"'Bout a year, I guess. Some of 'em left so quick they left kids behind."

"They left their kids. How do they live?"

"The kids?" He shrugged. "Best way they knows how, I guess."

I blinked. The world had tilted a little, and when I swallowed, my stomach left its bitter taste in my mouth. A great tiredness came over me, drink and all the riding, and grief, and I wondered what would happen when I stood up, if I'd have the strength to walk back to my brothers. I'd made a fool of myself, and I wondered what it would cost me.

I flinched as a shot rang out.

"Where's the sheriff?"

"Left with everybody else. There's a group getting together today, businessmen from out east, want to clear the land and sell it off for farming. Heard tell they'd bring in a lawman if the deal goes through."

"It's good farmland," I said.

"That it is."

"What do you do here?"

"Me?" He looked at me, as if I'd asked a dumb question. "I lives here."

"No," I said, blinking again, as the world began a nasty turning. "How do you live?"

"I works for the man who owns this here store. I was just starting to figure out where I'd go, maybe up to Nebraska, when I hears these businessmen had plans. If they work out, they be needing a store. So my boss man's waiting around to see. I'm waiting with him."

"Where do you live?"

He threw a thumb over his shoulder. "In the back."

"Where you from?"

He leaned forward in his chair, took the pipe from his mouth, and stared like he'd just discovered it. Then he looked at me with his eyebrows up.

"You from the newspaper?"

"No. Why?"

He shook his head. " 'Cause you the questionest-asking Negro I's ever seen in my life."

"I'm sorry," I said. "I didn't mean to pry. I . . ."

"Alabama."

"Excuse me?"

"I'm from Alabama." He cocked his head to one side,

listening. I listened with him, and heard a faint, steady thumping coming from inside the store.

"Begging your pardon," he said, "but I got to go see 'bout my daddy."

"Your daddy lives with you?"

He nodded.

I closed my eyes. How old was his father? What did he do?

"Can I see him?"

He looked at me, and his eyes were sharp.

"Ain't nothing he can . . ." he started, then cut off the thought. "If you wants to," he said, and got to his feet. I stood too quick and had to blink. I rubbed a hand across my face, and my beard surprised me.

The store had a musty smell, and most of the shelves were empty. The old man opened a door behind the last row of shelves and stood back to allow me to pass. The room had one window, through which a goodly portion of light showed. The oldest person I'd ever seen sat in one of the two cots that took up most of the room. He was wearing a white cotton nightshirt. His feet were bare, his hair and beard a dirty white. He was holding a broom, which he'd used to get his son's attention.

"Good morning, sir," I said, and the ancient one looked at me out of eyes glazed with fear and misunderstanding. As I waited for him to speak, he began a low growling, and his son moved forward, put a hand on his shoulder.

"Ain't no sense waiting for him to answer," he said. "He can't talk."

"Can't talk?"

He was rubbing the old man's shoulder, and I thought, *Look how gentle he is.*

He said, "Crackers cut his tongue out back in '59."

The room was turning. "For what?"

"Now it don't really matter for what, do it?" He looked at his father, who was growing more agitated by the minute. "I'll have to ask you to leave," he said. "You making him upset."

I backed into the store, made my unsteady way outside. I was thinking what kind of people would cut somebody's tongue out.

I walked down the street, through the sunless, rain-threatening day. I went inside the hotel. One of the whores was talking to a desolate-looking drifter. It looked like she was trying to get him to eat, and he'd made up his mind that food no longer mattered.

I sat at a table with my brothers. Halifax had my Winchester and saddlebag. I told him thank you. I told them I wanted to get out of this town as quickly as I could.

"You ready?" I asked. "This place gives me the creeps."

"It's all that whiskey you drank," Grafton said. "That and the night's activities."

I didn't say anything. I didn't want to think of the night's activities.

"We push on to Kansas," I said. "If we don't find them by then, I say we give it up and head back home. It ain't like we haven't tried."

For a moment neither of them answered, and I thought I was going to have a struggle.

Grafton said, "Hal and I had a talk with a man while you were gone. Businessman from back east. Said he and some partners was considering turning this whole area into farms. He said if that happened, the town would thrive again. We told him how we'd gone to Texas and all and drove a herd north, and how we were after some men who'd burned down our farm."

I looked at him. "So?"

"He asked if we were any good with guns, and we told him we weren't as good as you, but we could hold our own."

I waited.

"They're gonna need lawmen here, if the deal goes through. Hal and I sorta figured that once we got back from Kansas, we might come here. Get *paid* for shooting people. You know?" His smile did not look real.

"Lawmen?" I said. "We're farmers."

"You're a farmer," Halifax said. "Me and Grafton ain't never had it in us." He shrugged. "And it ain't forever. Just till we figure out what we want to do. You," he said, "know what you want to do."

I didn't like it. I'd opened my mouth to say so when the hotel door opened and men heavy with the dust of hard riding surged into the bar. Instantly, I was alert, counting. There were nine of them. The three men at the bar scattered when they approached.

"What you think?" Grafton said. "Think it's them?"

My heart was pounding. "There's a sure way to find out," I said. I stood up, too suddenly, and the world lurched. I closed my eyes until it steadied. I walked slowly across the room, stepped outside. Their horses were lined up, roped to hitching posts. They were breathing hard, lathered up. I saw the big horse, third from the end.

I went back inside. My heart was pounding. I sat down at the table.

"It's them," I said.

"You could have saved yourself a trip," Grafton said. "See the bareheaded guy? Third from the end. That's Caesar's medallion around his neck."

We sat there, not saying anything. One of the men called for something to eat.

"What do we do?" Halifax asked.

Grafton said, "Our plan was to get help from the sheriff."

"Ain't no sheriff," I said.

"Then we said we'd pay somebody to help us."

Halifax said harshly, "Who you going to find in this godforsaken town?"

"What about the man you talked to?" I asked. "Doesn't he have some partners?"

"He's a businessman," Halifax said. "Probably ain't never *held* a gun, much less pointed it at somebody."

"Why don't we ask him?"

"He's a *businessman*," Halifax said again. "From back east. Use your common sense."

I told him to keep his voice down. I was trying to think. I should have planned for this moment, so when it came, I wouldn't have to stop to figure. The men who'd killed my mama and Caesar were standing in front of me, and all I had to do was find our way to justice. But justice was nowhere to be found. The nearest sheriff I knew about was a half day's ride back east. There wasn't a man in this town fit even for a bounty hunter, and even if there were a half-dozen of them, I didn't have the time to round them up. I felt helpless. I started to think that the smart thing to do was to leave it alone, to let those men ride off to wherever it was they were going, and let our dreams of revenge die a natural death. I wanted to say that to my brothers, but when I said it to myself, I heard the way it sounded and I kept silent.

"We got no help," Grafton said.

"I say we just take 'em out," Halifax said.

Grafton said, "Be steady, brother. We said no killing."

"That's right," I said. "No killing."

"We just leave 'em?" Halifax hissed. "Just walk out of here and let 'em get away with what they done?"

I looked up. Both were looking at me, hard, waiting for my counsel. There was something moving both ways inside me, questions about what it meant to be a man, the deep desire for peace.

"Yes," I said. "We walk away from it. We said no more killing. I'm sick of killing. I know it's hard, but we let it go."

I put as much conviction in my voice as I could. Grafton looked at me without expression. A fury was building in Halifax's face.

"The hell we do," he hissed, and he pushed back from the table, knocking his chair to the floor and when he stood tall, his gun was in his hand.

"Halifax," I hollered, and I saw two of the men at the bar turn in curiosity, and Halifax was firing, and the men slumped, and blood was everywhere. Whores screamed, and the men who sat at the tables were diving for the floor. Halifax was still steady firing, and so was Grafton, and bottles were smashed behind the bar, and the killers were reaching for their guns. One of them shouted, "Niggers," and took a bullet between the eyes.

I froze, thinking two things, that I couldn't believe this was happening, and I didn't want to die. But if I wanted to live, freezing wasn't the way to do it. There was a voice inside me saying, "No, no, no," and I drew my gun. The air was alive with gunfire, and dense with the smell of smoke, and I was pumping shot after shot as fast as I could. In the little time I'd had to make up my mind, I'd intended to shoot to wound, but when it started, there wasn't time or space to be that careful, and because I wanted to live, I deliberately shot to kill. And though I was tired and still a little drunk, and scared, I felt something ease in me. I was through with being of two minds. I didn't want to kill, but now I had to. I would have preferred to walk out that door and leave those men the way we'd found them, but it hadn't worked out that way. I had to play the hand I'd been dealt, and I had to play it well, or me and my brothers were dead men. I shot fast and neat and I think I hit everything I aimed at.

And just like that, it was over, the smell of gunpowder mixed with the scent of blood, and another smell, which I recognized as death. I remembered what Bradford had said after the Indians had ambushed Steele, that it was like shooting fish in a barrel.

"Let's get out of here," I said.

"Watch your back," Grafton called to me.

I nodded. He was right. If we hadn't killed everybody, we might end up with a bullet in the back as we made our way out.

I motioned to my brothers to spread out, and we approached the bar, guns ready. We moved bodies with our boots, checking to see if anyone was still breathing. There were a lot of dead men on the floor, some sprawled on top of each other. No one was left alive.

"Okay," I said. "Let's go," and I spun, wondering where the sound came from that wasn't human. It was Halifax. He was shaking and whimpering. "Bastards," he said. "Unholy bastards," and he kicked at the pile of bodies, and began to fire into them, stopping to reload and fire again, all the while his steady, terrible cursing. I watched as if in a dream, and Grafton moved to stop him.

"No," I said. "Let him be."

"He's shooting dead men," Grafton said.

"Let him get it out of his system."

So that's what we did, let him get it out of his system, and he kept moving among the dead, firing and cursing, and now he'd begun to weep. Finally, he stopped, breathing hard, looked up at me and Grafton.

"It's okay," I said to him.

He looked at the dead men sprawled on the floor and what was on his face could only be described as peace, the deepest satisfaction.

"Well," he said. "I guess that lets out being lawmen."

I was shaking and calm at the same time, I was thinking and seeing as clear as I ever had. I walked over to the man who wore Caesar's medallion. He was on his side. There was a hole in his chest the size of a fist from which the blood still flowed. I reached and ripped the medallion from his neck, held it in my hand.

"Okay," I said. "Let's go."

We walked out of that hotel into the cloudy morning. We went down the street to get our horses, not hurrying, but with a purpose. I stood with my back to the table, gun ready, while the horses were saddled. Then I mounted up, and my brothers did, too, and we walked toward the edge of town. It wasn't until we were past the last building that I gave in to the urge, kicked my horse into a gallop and headed home.

Later, I'd still have two questions. First, who'd buried those men? Second, how long had the whole thing lasted? Thirty seconds, a minute? Two minutes? My brothers never wanted to talk about it, so I had no one to share my questions with, chief among which was why had the killing felt so good? I hated killing. But this time it felt like that jolt of morning whiskey taking effect after a night of drinking. The one that, even though it had caused the misery you were going through, brought with it the power to heal.

All of it was gone, the dizziness, the soreness in my body, the strange light the world seemed wrapped in, shame, and the nagging sense of a sure and fitting punish-

ment. I knew I needed some time to sort it out, and that
time had to be alone. I had to answer the biggest questions
of all: Was it killing that rid the sickness in my soul? And
how could I explain what I'd done to Amelia?

CHAPTER TWENTY-ONE

Three days of steady riding later, in the sunshine of late afternoon, we came to the hill and there was our farm below us. On the nights that we'd camped on our way back to the farm, my brothers and I had talked about what we would do now. I was heading back to Mexico to return Romero's money. After that I didn't know.

One thing was certain. Halifax and Grafton didn't want to be farmers. We talked about renting the farm out, but the truth was that none of us wanted to keep the connection of owning it, none of us wanted to be involved in the bad memory.

So we decided to sell it. Grafton and Halifax would do that while I was returning Romero's money. After that they'd take what they'd made from the drive and their share of the farm profits, and take off. There were lots of colored people in Nebraska. Maybe they'd go there and start a business. When I asked what kind of business, they said they didn't know.

There was a time when I'd have pushed them about making plans. I'd have given a speech about how life would swallow you up if you didn't know what you wanted to do, if you didn't take steps to prepare for it. I'd made that kind of speech before we headed to Texas. They hadn't known what they were going to do back then. For them, heading south to buy a herd of cattle and drive it north was nothing more than an adventure that would put money in their pockets.

In that way, they were like young men everywhere. Even though I was only a few years older, I was different. Sometimes I'd try to figure out if there was something I could look back and point to as the source of that difference. But I never found anything. Making plans was in me, like I'd been born to it, the way I'd been born to expecting the worst, and feeling lonely in the middle of a crowd. Even when I was a kid, I knew I was going to do something, make something of myself. I just didn't know until later what it would be. And when I found it, I was sure. It was my dream. Amelia had been at the center of that dream, but now I'd done things that meant she might not be.

I didn't make that speech to my brothers. I was in the same boat they were in. I had no clear-cut plans. I'd lost my capacity for dreaming. I'd lost the certainty that I'd had before I left for Texas. I couldn't depend on myself anymore to be who I thought I was, a good man who welcomed hard work as a way to gain what he wanted, who turned away from killing, who'd looked forward to a family, a long, peaceful life that left something behind for a line of Partlows that would stretch into the future.

We rode down the hill to the deserted farm. The doorframe was no longer standing. As we made our way through the ruin, I found myself hoping for a miracle. Even though my mother and Caesar were buried in fresh graves behind Amelia's barn, I looked for signs of them.

The sunlight was bright and thin, and the Missouri air

was seasoned with bird flight and darting insects. As I squinted against the light, I remembered my growing up here. I remembered my mama's smile, and how she'd raised us to be good men, her without a man, but she did it. And then Caesar coming, and all that he'd taught me, and how he'd been a father without ever using the word.

Now when I squinted, I was squeezing back the tears. I'd left here six months ago feeling whole and unafraid and determined. I had a sense of myself as a good man whose head was on right, who went out into the world feeling safe. I wanted to feel safe again. I wanted to be back in my mama's house as a boy, with the smell of cooking coming from the kitchen, and my brothers out playing in the yard, and Caesar teaching me how to move soundlessly through the woods, and not to shoot at anything I didn't mean to kill. All of that was gone now. I'd gone into the world. I'd held my dream before me, like a shield. And life had smashed it.

Maybe no one was safe, maybe no one would ever be. Maybe a dream was just what it said it was, something you made up out of nothing, something that came in the night and was gone when you woke in the morning.

Way across the fields I heard a bell ring, calling a family to supper. My brothers and I were still on our horses. Grafton came over to me where I sat staring into the remains of the barn's foundation.

"You about ready to go?" he asked.

I nodded.

"Me and Halifax been talking," he said. "We'll go into town tonight. Stay there. In the morning, we can go about the job of trying to sell the place. Ain't no need in putting it off."

I said okay.

"You'll stay at Amelia's?"

"I guess so," I said.

"You ready?"

"I guess so," I said. "Grafton?"

"What?"

"What we done . . . you think it was right?"

"I don't know. I just know it's done." He looked out over the fallow field. "I'm not like you, Josh. I don't spend time wondering once I've done it. It's just done, and I'll deal with whatever."

"I only want to do right," I said.

"I know," he answered. "But maybe you ask too much of yourself. Maybe nobody can do right all the time."

Amelia was in the yard as we approached, weeding the flower garden, and she looked up. Even from the distance, I could see the light turn on in her face. Halifax and Grafton hung back, and I kicked my horse and cantered forward, skidded to a stop, and swung from the saddle. Amelia was coming toward me, arms open, face half-crying, half-laughing, and all of it seemed unreal. I was trying to figure out what I was feeling, and then she was in my arms, and Lord, she felt good, and I was holding her, her face buried in my neck.

"You're back," she said.

"Yes."

She pulled away from me. "Let me look at you."

I let her look, and I was thinking that it wouldn't take her more than a second to be able to tell what I'd done. But she just kept smiling.

"You grew a beard," she said. "It's so good to see you. It was harder waiting for you this time than when you went to Texas. Isn't that something?"

She looked over her shoulder and called a greeting to Halifax and Grafton, who hadn't got off their horses.

"They're going into town," I said. "They'll stay there for a while."

"They're welcome to stay here. Halifax. Grafton. You know you're welcome."

They said they knew that and thank you very much, but they'd take her up on her hospitality another time.

I told them I'd meet up with them in the morning and they said "See you later," and rode off down the road. We watched until they disappeared, our arms around each other.

"You hungry?" she asked. I knew she was dying to ask what had happened, but she'd wait until the time was right.

"Yes," I said. "But first I want to take a bath."

"Want to come in the house? Mom and Dad are visiting the Littles. Mrs. Little came down with a fever. They'll be back later on tonight."

"No," I said. "The barn'll be fine."

"You got clean clothes in your saddlebag?"

"No. I'm not sure I know what clean clothes are."

"I'll get some of Dad's."

"Just a shirt will be fine."

She smiled. "If you're going to get clean, get clean all the way."

"Okay," I said. "Bring me some britches, too."

Maybe it was just me, but it felt like we were being careful, talking to one another the way strangers did, polite and normal on the outside, but cautious underneath. We went to the barn, and I took the tin tub down from where it hung on a nail on the wall. Amelia went into the house to put water on to heat, and while she was gone I unsaddled my horse and fed and watered him.

Then I helped Amelia carry the water to the barn, pour it into the tub. She went back into the house while I washed away the dust and fever and death, and the feel of the whore from my body. When I finished, I put on her father's clean white shirt, and it fit, and I put on his britches which were just a little short and full in the waist, but still okay. The clothes smelled good. It had been a long time since I'd worn something that had been washed in real soap by a woman.

When I'd dressed, I went out back to where my mother lay next to Caesar. Somebody had put fresh flowers on the graves, and I sat a while in silence, looking out over the field, the trees that ringed it, and I didn't feel funny about talking to the dead.

"Well, Mom, Caesar, we found them. They won't be burning any more farms. They won't be killing any more innocent people."

I felt tears come to my eyes, and I blinked them back. I reached in my pocket, pulled out Caesar's medallion. I looped the leather thong over my head and let the medallion rest outside my shirt.

"I hope you won't be too disappointed with me. You didn't teach me to be a killer, either one of you. But I have killed, and every time I did it was because I had to. I'd like to go someplace where killing don't exist, but I don't know if there is such a place in this whole wide country.

"But I'm all right. I'm not happy with what I done, but I've made my peace with it. I hope what I told you don't cause you to rest uneasy."

"Josh?"

I jumped! I hadn't heard Amelia come up behind me. I turned. She had the expression of a person trying not to frown.

"You ready for something to eat?"

I nodded.

"Come inside."

I got up and followed her into the house, and she was

looking at my chest out of the corner of her eye. She sat me down at the kitchen table, and began making my dinner. When she pulled up a chair across from me, I was facing a plate of fried chicken, potato salad, green beans, and corn bread. In the middle of the table was a pitcher of lemonade. It was so cold the glass had beads of moisture sliding down its sides. I dug a fork in, raised it to my mouth.

"Say your grace," she said.

A little embarrassed, I bowed my head. For a moment, I couldn't think of a single blessing. I'd blessed my food before eating all my life until I got to Texas. But now the only thing that came into my head was "Jesus wept."

She was looking at me with a funny smile, the way people looked at a child who cried out in the middle of a preacher's sermon.

"Out of the habit?"

Her eyes dropped to the medallion at my chest, and when she raised them they held a question different from the one she'd asked.

"I guess so," I mumbled.

"Dear Lord," she prayed. "Please bless this food that we are about to receive for the nourishment of our bodies, in Christ's name, amen."

I said, "I remember that one."

She was still smiling that funny smile. "Eat."

So I began to eat, and she started chattering away, and her eyes kept darting to my chest. She said how dry the summer had been, and there was a new family that had moved in a couple of miles down the road between here and town. They had six children, and the girls were the cutest little things, and so on and so forth.

Then she said, "That's Caesar's medallion."

"That it is."

"So tell me what happened."

"When?"

"The past twelve days. You left looking for the men who killed your mother and Caesar. If that medallion means anything, you found them."

I didn't say anything.

"Did you find them?"

"We did."

"And what happened?"

I looked into the wilderness of the food on my plate. "It was about half a day's ride from the Kansas border," I said. "Place called Elmertown. Couple of years ago somebody discovered gold there, and the town built up around it. The gold ran out, and now it's a couple of days short of being a ghost town. That might change. A bunch of guys from out East rode in while we were there. Looking into turning the land around the town into farms. They ought to be able to make a go off it. It's good land."

"What," Amelia asked, "happened to those men you were after?" She was trying to be calm and steady, but her voice was tight.

So here it was. I looked directly into her face. It was drawn, as tight as her voice.

"Tell me something," I said.

"Okay."

"If there was something you wanted to know, and somebody could show you that not knowing wouldn't make any difference in the long run, and that knowing could do you harm, would you still want to?"

"That depends on what it's about. If it's about you, and it's important, I'd want to know."

"How do you tell when something's important?"

" 'Cause it finds a place inside you. It won't leave you alone. Every time you turn around it's there waiting to be tended to."

"Give me an example."

"Truth," she said. "Truth is important. Especially between two people who plan to make a life together. You can't have that without truth."

"We killed them," I said. "Me and Halifax and Grafton. We killed them."

She tried to take it like a man, but she couldn't. She brought both hands to her chest, palms together. Her eyes got real wide, then she closed them.

I tried to figure out what I was feeling, but all I could recognize was tired and sad in the face of danger. It was like standing at the bottom of a hill and a boulder coming down at me, and where was I going to find the strength to move?

"How did it happen?"

"They walked into this hotel where we'd stayed the night. I went outside to check the horses. You remember one was on this real big horse? When I got back, Grafton said that one of them had Caesar's medallion around his neck.

"We'd planned to go for the sheriff, but it was our luck to be in a town that didn't have one. The second plan was to hire some men, bounty hunters, to help us take them in. But there wasn't much pickings in the way of men.

"The place was strange that way. It felt like a town that collected defeated men, a place where you went to die. Even the smell said that.

"Anyway, me and Grafton were talking about what we were going to do, and all of a sudden Halifax was shooting. Wasn't nothing for me to do but start shooting too if I wanted to stay alive. It was over in less time than it takes to tell it."

"Did you find out why they'd done what they had?"

I shook my head. "Wasn't no time for talking."

"How did you feel?"

"The truth?"

She nodded.

"I had two feelings that came together and confused me. I felt sorry about it, like I was dirty and worthless. But at the same time, I felt good. I'd had some kind of sickness, fever and all, and after that it went away."

She was staring at me.

"You might as well know all of it," I said. "They wasn't the first I killed. We got attacked by a couple of bounty hunters up in Abilene. They killed one of my hands and Halifax's girl. They opened up on us, and I fired to kill."

"Halifax had a girl?"

I nodded. "Met her in Laredo. He was bringing her home to meet mama. She was a good person, just as pretty as can be."

"What was she doing in Laredo?"

I paused. "Working."

"Doing what?"

"She was a whore."

"A whore."

"Yes."

"Halifax was bringing home a whore?"

"At first I felt the same way you did," I said. "Then my feelings changed. It's a lot more complicated than it sounds."

I could tell from her face that it wasn't complicated for her. Not yet. But I knew it was going to be.

She asked, "Why were bounty hunters after you?"

"Halifax got in some trouble in Laredo for something he didn't do, and when we broke him out of jail, he killed a sheriff."

"You were busy in Texas," she said. "Finding whores to bring home. Killing sheriffs."

"It wasn't me who did either one of those. But I agree it don't sound good."

"Doesn't sound good? Is that how you'd describe it?"

"I mean it ain't so simple as it sounds."

"And that makes it okay, because it wasn't simple?"

"It was you," I said, "who wanted to know the truth."

"What happened to the sweet man who left to go to Texas? Who wanted to buy a herd so we could go off and be together. What happened to him?"

I thought it was a good question. It was the same one I'd been asking myself.

"He went out into the world," I said. "He discovered America."

"The next thing you'll be telling me is that you slept with whores."

I'd had enough of this truth stuff. "I won't be telling you that because I didn't."

And then she began to cry. Not loud, but deep, and tears ran down her face.

"I'm sorry, Amelia," I said.

"The worst part of it is that you're not sorry. You talk about killing as if you were born to it. There's no regret in you."

"Don't think there's no regret. There's enough of that for a lifetime."

"I'm no fool," she said. "I didn't expect that you'd never run into trouble. I worried about you and your brothers, colored men going off to do what you were doing. I knew there'd be danger, times you'd have to protect yourself with guns, yes, maybe even kill someone. I understand a little about the world, Joshua, even if I've never been out of Missouri. But I never expected you to tell me that killing felt good, that killing healed you.''

''I didn't say it healed me. And the good feeling didn't last. But the sickness did go away. I'm not saying killing made it go away.

''And I did feel good at the time. I don't feel good now. Just settled about it. I thought it was making peace with it, but there ain't no peace. Just accepting. I done it, and I accept it. I wish I hadn't. I wish I hadn't had to. But I haven't changed that way. I don't want to fire a gun at a man ever again in my life. I choose to live in peace.''

''Did you ask for forgiveness?''

''From who?''

''God.''

''Not yet,'' I said.

''You've changed.''

''I guess I have, Amelia. I guess I have. And I need to take the time to figure out just how.''

''What do we do now, Josh?''

''I'm going to Mexico. I've got to pay a man some money.''

''Can I go with you?''

''It's not safe. And the truth is, I need time to be alone, to think through things.''

''Like what?''

''All of it,'' I said.

''Are you coming back?''

''Yes.''

''I've been living for the day when we'd be together. You said we'd go to Montana. You said . . . Why didn't you think of me?''

It came out a whisper, long and thin and grieving.

''Amelia,'' I said. ''I thought of you all the time.''

I could see the effort she was making to pull herself

together, to not whine, or break down in front of me.

"I'm going to lie down," she said. "I'll leave you to eat in peace."

She got up and smoothed her dress, touched a hand to her cheek. She moved as if she would come toward me, and I saw her pull her body back, and she turned and went from the room.

I sat looking into my plate, the half-eaten chicken, the place where my fork had carved into the hill of potato salad. I wasn't hungry anymore. I poured a glass of lemonade. It was sweet and sour at the same time and I felt the insides of my cheeks pucker. I looked out the window into the yard, and then I got up and scraped my plate and left it in the kitchen tub. I went outside and sat next to the graves of Caesar and my mama, and tried to think of nothing.

I heard Amelia's parents when they came back from visiting the neighbors, but I didn't go to meet them. I sat there, watching evening fall. The night came alive with fireflies, the swoop of bats, an owl call off in the distance. When the mosquitoes descended upon me, the stars were out in full force. I got up and went into the barn. I made a pallet for myself on a bed of straw. I stretched out on my back and stared up at where the barn roof disappeared in darkness, and although I didn't think I would, finally I slept.

Amelia woke me in the night. Slid beneath the cover and pressed her body to mine. At first I was surprised, but then I remember thinking that nothing again in life would surprise me. Things might sneak up on me, catch me unawares, but I felt that when I considered them, I wouldn't be surprised.

"Amelia," I said.

"Please, don't talk, Josh. Just hold me."

So I held her, thinking what would happen if her father came upon us, how would I explain, and then she was doing things I couldn't ignore.

"Amelia, don't," I said.

She didn't answer.

I knew that if I didn't do something right away, there'd be no stopping. I pulled away from her, sat up, held her hands. I could barely make out her face. Her eyes were closed, and I could feel her trembling.

"I don't want to lose you," she said.

"You're not going to lose me. But if you don't get up and go back to the house, you're going to hate yourself. This isn't who you are."

I heard it in her voice. It was anger or frustration, or both. "What makes you think you know who I am?"

"Amelia, go back in the house. Please."

"You're not coming back, are you?"

"I'm coming back, Amelia. I swear it."

"What did I do?"

"You didn't do anything."

"I won't beg."

"I don't want you to."

For a moment, there was a silence so deep and so long I found myself listening to it. She sighed, leaned forward, kissed me on the cheek, sisterly.

"Good-bye, Joshua. Take care of yourself."

I said I would. She got up, left as silently as she'd come. I sat there in the darkness, thinking of what had happened, wondering if I was a fool. The truth was I didn't know. I felt like the world was full of questions and I was stuck in the middle of it without an answer to my name.

I lay there for a while, and then I got up, put my boots on, saddled my horse in the dark. I got my rifle and my saddlebag, opened the barn door, walked my horse outside.

I swung into the saddle and headed past the silent house, away from the graves of my loved ones. I'd meet my brothers in town, get money from the bank, and head to Mexico to pay Romero back. I'd take the time to try to figure things out.

When I reached the road, I stiffened. Someone was coming toward me out of the darkness. I reached for my gun, held it across my lap. When the rider got close enough for me to make him out, I couldn't believe it.

"I got here as soon as I could," Bradford said. "I heard you had some trouble."

"How'd you hear?"

"Family you spent the night with. Staked a claim across the way from my mama's."

"So they made it," I said.

"Yup. What about you? That your farm I passed?"

"It is," I said. "I took some losses, but the trouble's taken care of."

"So," he said. "I guess I made this trip for nothing." A cock crowed, and his horse shifted.

I asked, "Did you hear about that gang?"

"Word traveled," he said.

"You hear anything about who they were, why they were doing what they did?"

He shook his head.

I blinked, disappointed. I'd had the feeling that knowing would have made a difference.

Bradford asked, "Where you headed?"

"To town. Stop at the bank. Then south."

"Last I heard, Montana's the other way."

"Going to Mexico. Got to pay a man I owe. I don't need Romero on my trail."

"I know what you mean. Need some company?"

"You got nothing else to do?"

"I didn't say I had nothing to do. I asked if you needed some company."

"I see," I said. "Well, now that you mention it, company would be just fine." I couldn't keep from grinning. "It sure is good to see you."

"We'll see how long that lasts," he said. "Let's move out," and a rooster called again, and the day was dawning. I turned to look at the house where Amelia lay sleeping. I said a silent promise to return, to head with her to Montana and make our dream come true. Then I spoke to my horse, and me and Bradford took off on our way to Mexico.

THE TRAIL DRIVE SERIES
by Ralph Compton

From St. Martin's Paperbacks

The only riches Texas had left after the Civil War were five million maverick longhorns and the brains, brawn and boldness to drive them north to where the money was. Now, Ralph Compton brings this violent and magnificent time to life in an extraordinary epic series based on the history-blazing trail drives.

BEFORE THE LEGEND, THERE WAS THE MAN...

AND A POWERFUL DESTINY TO FULFILL.

On October 26, 1881, three outlaws lay dead in a dusty vacant lot in Tombstone, Arizona. Standing over them—Colts smoking—were Wyatt Earp, his two brothers Morgan and Virgil, and a gun-slinging gambler named Doc Holliday. The shootout at the O.K. Corral was over—but for Earp, the fight had just begun...

WYATT EARP

MATT BRAUN

In 1889, Bill Tilghman joined the historic land rush that transformed a raw frontier into Oklahoma Territory. A lawman by trade, he set aside his badge to make his fortune in the boomtowns. Yet Tilghman was called into service once more, on a bold, relentless journey that would make his name a legend for all time—in an epic confrontation with outlaw Bill Doolin.

OUTLAW KINGDOM

MATT BRAUN

OUTLAW KINGDOM
Matt Braun
_____ 95618-5 $5.99 U.S./$6.99 CAN.